"I'm asking you to give me a week my way, and then if I haven't convinced you, I'll try yours,"
Alexa said.

Ian's eyebrows crunched together. "A week?"

"I need to get to know her. Her likes and dislikes. Her dreams."

"I can tell you those. And although I want you to like Jana, I didn't hire you to be her new best friend. You're the tutor. I'll still be involved a little in her education. I promised her I wouldn't totally abandon her."

The force of his voice faded slightly at the end of the last sentence, making Alexa wonder what was behind those words. Again that connection sprang up, and she wanted to help him any way she could with his daughter. He had a way of peering at her that sparked something deep inside her.

He looked away and stared out the window behind the teacher's desk. Finally after a long minute, he swung his full attention back to her. "I'll give you a day."

Books by Margaret Daley

Love Inspired

The Power of Love
Family for Keeps
Sadie's Hero
The Courage to Dream
What the Heart Knows
A Family for Tory
*Gold in the Fire
*A Mother for Cindy
*Light in the Storm
The Cinderella Plan
*When Dreams Come True

*Tidings of Joy
**Once Upon a Family
**Heart of the Family
**Family Ever After
A Texas Thanksgiving
**Second Chance Family
**Together for the Holidays
†Love Lessons

*The Ladies of Sweetwater Lake
**Fostered by Love
†Helping Hands Homeschooling

Love Inspired Suspense

Hearts on the Line
Heart of the Amazon
So Dark the Night
Vanished
Buried Secrets

Don't Look Back
Forsaken Canyon
What Sarah Saw
Poisoned Secrets
Cowboy Protector

MARGARET DALEY

feels she has been blessed. She has been married more than thirty years to her husband, Mike, whom she met in college. He is a terrific support and her best friend. They have one son, Shaun. Margaret has been writing for many years and loves to tell a story. When she was a little girl, she would play with her dolls and make up stories about their lives. Now she writes these stories down. She especially enjoys weaving stories about families and how faith in God can sustain a person when things get tough. When she isn't writing, she is fortunate to be a teacher for students with special needs. Margaret has taught for more than twenty years and loves working with her students. She has also been a Special Olympics coach and has participated in many sports with her students.

Love Lessons
Margaret Daley

Steeple
Hill®

Published by Steeple Hill Books™

STEEPLE HILL BOOKS

Steeple
Hill®

Recycling programs
for this product may
not exist in your area.

ISBN-13: 978-0-373-87590-0

LOVE LESSONS

www.SteepleHill.com

Printed in U.S.A.

For if ye forgive men their trespasses,
your heavenly Father will also forgive you.
—*Matthew* 6:14

To all parents who have homeschooled
their children.

Chapter One

"Don't die on me."

Alexa Michaels patted the dashboard of her twelve-year-old car as it chugged toward its destination, only a half a block away.

At least the car had gotten her to the street where she needed to go, and she was thirty minutes early to her interview for the tutoring position. The vehicle bellowed a plume of smoke from its tailpipe, the wind whisking it away as it sputtered past another sizable dwelling. Finally, her car died two houses away from her objective, a single-story Mediterranean home on an acre.

She pushed the car door open. Its creaking sound protested the action. With a sigh, she retrieved her large purse from the floor and stood. A brisk breeze caught her long, multicolored skirt and whipped it about her legs. Holding it down while clutching her bag, she hurried toward the house.

Halfway up the sidewalk to the front entrance, a plastic liter bottle fell from the sky and splattered two feet from her, clear liquid splashing and wetting the bottom of her skirt.

What in the world!

Stunned, she stopped, her purse slipping from her fingers to plop on the concrete next to her, the bag's contents pouring all over the ground. She stooped to scoop up her items—lipstick, cell, brush, pen...

A man charged around the side of the house and hurried toward her. Jumping up, she took a step back, the few personal objects in her hand landing in the pile on the ground.

Maybe I've got the wrong place. Maybe I should leave...

Then she saw a young girl appear, not far behind the man, and relaxed, taking stock of the pair as they approached. Tall, lean, the male's long-legged stride ate up the distance between them quickly. His tanned features were set in a look of concern, but as his gaze roamed down her length, his eyes widened briefly before he managed to school his expression into a neutral one.

He came to a halt, pushing his wire-rimmed glasses up his nose, framing beautiful Nordic blue eyes with long black eyelashes. "Are you all right? The rocket didn't hit you, did it?"

With her gaze held captive by his, the questions barely registered on her mind.

"Were you hit?" the man asked again.

She mentally shook herself out of the daze and focused on what he'd said. "No. It just splashed my skirt." She peered at the smashed liter bottle. "What was in it?"

"Only water."

The girl who looked about ten years old, with copper-colored hair pulled back in a ponytail, skidded to a stop next to the man. "I can't believe it went over the house, Dad. That was awesome!" She threw her arms around her father, not seeming to notice Alexa.

Returning the hug, he peered down at his daughter, grinning. "Yeah, definitely the best one yet. You did good."

At that moment a gust of wind sent Alexa's skirt dancing about her legs and played with her long mane, whipping it across her face. She reached down, grabbing up as much of the rayon fabric as she could while trying to keep her hair out of her eyes.

Hunched over, Alexa looked up through her curly strands at the man whose own short, black hair stayed in perfect place, complementing the impeccable clothes he wore, tan slacks, navy blue long-sleeved shirt and a jacket. "I'm here for the interview."

"You're early." He turned his grin on her and stuck out his hand. "You must be Alexa Michaels. I'm Ian Ferguson and this one—" he nodded toward the child "—is my daughter, Jana."

His smile lit his whole face and reached deep into his eyes. It set her heart to beating fast until she noticed the way Jana had stepped a little behind her father, gripping him tighter. Was the girl really that uncomfortable around strangers?

Straightening and hoping her skirt stayed down, Alexa fit her hand in his and shook it. The touch of his fingers around hers made her pulse speed up, but she quickly regained control. Being attracted to a potential employer wasn't in her plans. She needed this job.

When he looked at her quizzically, she squashed her reaction to the man and returned his grin. "I wasn't sure if my car would make it. I came early in case I had to walk some." She returned her attention to the child. "It's nice to meet you, Jana."

The young girl smiled, but it didn't stay on her face long. However, her wary gaze remained on Alexa as though she wasn't quite sure what to make of the situation.

"You like to do experiments?" Alexa tried again to connect with the child.

Jana nodded. "Yes. They're fun. Like this one." She gestured toward the liter rocket.

"Great, I do, too."

"We were testing different ways to make a rocket go up," Ian explained. "We used water and compressed air." He winced. "It went too well. If we do that one again, we'll have to go out into the country. Again, I'm sorry about nearly hitting you with the bottle. Our first four attempts weren't nearly as successful." He scanned the street in front of his house, then his driveway. "Where is your car?"

"It died." Alexa gestured toward the neighbor's curb. "It's over there."

"Come inside. We'll talk while Jana cleans up the rocket experiment in the backyard, then we'll decide what to do about your dead car."

Alexa squatted to gather her purse contents and stuff them into her bag. A lingering tinge of heat still scored her cheeks. His gaze had flared slightly when it had landed on her beat-up vehicle in need of being painted, especially where the rust showed. Most people who saw her car wondered how it even ran. Sometimes she did, too.

Before she could finish, Ian knelt next to her, grabbed her apple and brush on the grass and gave them to her. "You have a lot in that purse." The last item on the ground by his feet was a romance paperback. He picked it up and studied the cover. "Interesting."

She wasn't going to blush anymore. She enjoyed reading a good love story. After she took the book from him, she dropped it into her purse with the rest of the returned items. "I like to be prepared for all situations. You never know when you'll be stuck in a line. I get a lot of my reading done while waiting."

After rising, he offered her his hand. She grasped it and stood, trying to ignore the strong feel of his fingers around hers and the tingling that zipped up her arm. His firm grasp conveyed a confident man. Their gazes connected for a moment, and a rush of warmth continued its path through her. She quickly tugged her hand to her side.

Pivoting, he started for his stucco house, glanced back when she didn't move and said, "Coming?"

Still stunned by that brief connection, she managed to murmur, "Oh, sorry. Yes." What in the world was wrong with her?

Shaking her hand as though that would rid her mind of the sensations of the brief contact, she hurriedly caught up and walked beside him toward the double glass doors and the front porch. Ian Ferguson walked in and waved her through. She stepped into a spacious raised foyer. Through the back bank of windows, Alexa saw the small lake that several of the houses in the area abutted.

"Have a seat in the living room while I check on Jana." He headed across the sunken living room and mounted the couple of steps into a large kitchen.

As Alexa heard the murmur of low voices, she took a seat on the edge of a pristine white couch and put her over-size purse on the floor next to her feet. Her fingers grazed across the soft leather of the sofa. Very expensive, if the pliant feel meant anything.

The formal, tidy room screamed a warning: no kids allowed. She hoped she hadn't tracked in any dirt. She checked the path she'd taken and breathed a sigh of relief at the clean white area rug where she'd treaded.

The sound of voices had stopped. When she swung her

gaze toward the kitchen, it fell upon Ian Ferguson standing in the doorway, studying her. A gasp escaped her lips, and as much as she wished she didn't, a blush seared her cheeks—again.

"Sorry if I surprised you." He folded his long length onto a black leather chair across from her and laid a folder in his lap. "Sometimes my daughter gets distracted and forgets to do what she's supposed to."

Don't all kids? Alexa kept that comment to herself. "Does she enjoy science?"

"One of her favorite subjects." He relaxed back. "What subject do you enjoy the most?"

"If I were smart, I'd say science, but it isn't. I do love anything to do with animals, though." She tried to loosen the tightness that gripped her, but she couldn't shake the sensation she was in a sterile environment of black and white that she needed to keep that way at all costs.

One thick, dark brow arched. "So what are your favorite subjects to teach?"

"English and history, though I have a gift for languages. I thought about being a secondary-school English teacher, but finally decided I love young kids too much so I chose elementary education. I'm starting my last year of college this semester. I can't take a full load of classes, but I hope to finish by May next year." *Just a few years later than my peers.*

"Your college adviser had glowing things to say about you. Dr. Baker is a friend. She said you're her top student."

"I've enjoyed her classes and was elated when she became my adviser." And friend. Nancy Baker had been responsible for her getting her last job as a nanny and for telling her about this job.

I want this to work out. Lord, I may need Your assistance here.

He picked up the folder, opened it and scanned a piece of paper. "Your résumé mentions you were a nanny for the Petersons up until last month. What happened?"

"Mr. Peterson's company transferred him to Houston. They moved there at the end of December." Which stuck her with finding another job. She was temporarily working at a restaurant, but being a waitress wasn't where her heart was.

"The past three days I've been interviewing some other applicants from an agency. I'll make up my mind this weekend. I need help as soon as possible."

Alexa heard a door shutting and then voices from the kitchen. According to Dr. Baker, Ian wasn't married. Who else was in the house besides the daughter? "Dr. Baker told me you're a CPA and with tax season coming up, you'll need help temporarily with Jana's schooling."

"I was able to manage teaching her and running my business from home until lately. But now, I need someone to work with Jana on her studies, continuing where I've left off. I'll still be involved as much as my job will allow, but for the next four months that won't be a lot."

The fact he was a single dad trying to be both parents touched Alexa. Across the room, their gazes linked, and for a brief moment her mind blanked. Finally she glanced toward the kitchen, the sound of a girl's voice resonating through the air. "How old is Jana?"

"She's ten. She'll be eleven in two months, and she's counting down the days."

Again she looked directly at Ian Ferguson, the blue of his eyes startling behind his glasses, an intensity, full of seriousness, pouring off him. "May I ask why Jana is being homeschooled?"

"My daughter has struggled with school anxiety—no, it's more than that. It's separation anxiety, and she hasn't attended since the end of August. In fact, she has problems sometimes even leaving our property."

Even with the little she knew about separation anxiety, Alexa realized there was a lot more to the story. But the firm set of his jaw indicated there wouldn't be any more information given out. "Does Jana like to write?"

"That and science are her favorite subjects."

"Good, even at a young age I encourage children to write. What does she hate to do?"

One corner of his mouth lifted, a dimple in his right cheek. "Math. She probably won't be following in my footsteps. She actually struggles in the subject, and I'm afraid my patience isn't what it should be when I teach something that comes easy for me." When his grin broadened, his whole face brightened, and laugh lines fanned outward from his eyes. The sparkle in those blue depths gave the impression of shared understanding.

But that was just an illusion. Alexa couldn't find anything they had in common. For starters, a room like the one she was in would give her hives if she stayed in it long, whereas the man across from her appeared as though he fit easily into a formal setting. "I have some games to help kids learn math. It wasn't easy for me when I was growing up, so I certainly understand what Jana is going through."

"Do you have any questions about the job?"

"No, Dr. Baker explained what you need. I'll be starting my spring semester at college in a couple of weeks. I take classes in the evenings and will have to leave by four on Tuesdays and Thursdays."

"What kind of teaching schedule would you maintain?"

"I like to seize the moment, especially in a one-on-one setting. If something comes up that piques Jana's interest, I'll use that and run with it. If she saw a TV show about, say, dogs and was interested in a certain breed, then we'd do a unit around that breed. Start with the child's interests and go from there is my motto."

"How about that math she hates?"

"We'd get to it. She just may not realize it at first. I can incorporate some math into other units—disguise it somewhat so she doesn't realize she's learning math."

Ian blinked rapidly then dropped his gaze to his lap. "I'm still checking out references and interviewing. But I'll have an answer by Saturday." He rose. "Now, let's check on your car. I can try to start it. If it won't work, I'll give you a ride home."

Alexa stood. "We don't need to check on it. It won't start. My cousin works for a garage. He'll have to come tow it to the shop. This has happened before. My car has lived past its life expectancy thanks to my cousin. And if the Lord is willing, it will be resurrected for another couple of thousand miles."

"And if not?"

She chuckled. "I'm in big trouble. All my extra money goes to finishing school. What's life without a few bumps in the road? I'm not gonna worry about it until I have no other choice."

"Let me go tell Jana and my housekeeper, Madge, I'm taking you home."

"Are you sure? I can call a cab. It sounds like you have a lot of work to do."

"I'm sure. I have to run a couple of errands, and Madge will be here for a few more hours. She's only part-time. She comes Tuesdays and Thursdays."

Did that explain the super-neat house, or was it because of the man before her? She suspected the answer was the man. "Then I accept the ride."

* * *

Alexa pushed the car door open. "Thanks for the ride home."

"No problem. I'll call you one way or another about the job." Ian sent her a smile, which she returned as she slid from the front seat.

When she left and strolled toward her duplex, his gaze traveled upward from her gold flats to her flowery patterned skirt of every bright color in the spectrum, to her heavy orange sweater that covered a sunshine-yellow turtleneck underneath. He stopped for a few seconds at her mahogany hair that fell in a mass of curls halfway down her back. Beautiful but wild, which he guessed was due to the wind. Her light scent of vanilla hung in the air, a reminder even after she'd left that she'd been in his car. His memory of her sloe-eyed gaze, so dark it was almost black, prodded him to give her a chance at the job. For a moment in the living room, their eyes had touched, and he hadn't been able to deny the sense of connection. Which was why he was leery.

He'd decided on the ride to her place not to hire her. As she'd talked earlier at his house and in the car, he'd realized she was too different from what he was used to. And too young. He'd learned, painfully, opposites didn't really attract. His ex-wife and he had gone in different directions since they had gotten married. He wouldn't make that mistake again.

Although he wouldn't have to be around Alexa much, her whimsical attitude would drive him up the wall in less than a week. What teacher didn't have lesson plans? Okay, she was still studying to be a teacher and maybe she hadn't gotten to that part. But still surely structure and organization were important to any teacher. And having a routine was definitely important for Jana. That was what had kept them both sane these past few months doing something he'd never dreamed he would do. That and the Helping Hands Homeschooling Group.

No, he'd go with the first candidate he interviewed two days before—a retired teacher whom the agency had sent. A young woman just wouldn't give Jana the stability she needed right now in her life. Jana's world had been rocked when her mother walked out on them fourteen months ago, a couple of weeks before Thanksgiving. She hadn't even called her daughter on her last birthday or at Christmas. She'd only sent lavish presents with a signed card and a brief note, as if that were enough. The Fergusons—father and daughter—definitely didn't need another flighty, irresponsible woman in their lives.

As he turned into a parking lot at a strip mall, his grip on the steering wheel tightened until pain streaked up his arms. Tracy had left him for another man and obviously didn't even care about her own daughter. What kind of God would do that to a little girl whose world used to revolve around her mother?

Half an hour later Ian returned home after finishing his two errands. His daughter stood at the door to the garage waiting for him. After each interview, Jana had given her opinion of the candidate and none of them had pleased her. She wasn't happy with him having to work more. She craved his attention, and was wary of strangers. He certainly understood why after her mother abandoned her—and him—for a man Jana had never met.

"Hey, pumpkin." Ian entered the house, the scent of dinner teasing his senses. "Ah, Madge is making her lasagna for us. I love Tuesdays and Thursdays when she's here to cook dinner."

"Yep, your cooking isn't exactly up to her standards."

"I'd have to take classes for years to be up to her standards." Another job he'd had to take over when his wife left. At least he'd graduated from putting prepared dinners in the oven to heat up to actually following a simple recipe.

"I asked her for lasagna because nothing is going right. Well, except the rocket launch." His daughter's mouth twisted into a pout. "I don't want anyone else to teach me."

"I can't do it all right now. It's only until the end of April. Not a life sentence."

"I'll work on my own when you need me to. I promise."

"Your education is too important to me to leave it to random chance." Sighing, he made his way to the family room and sat on the couch. He might be sorry, but he asked, "Which one of the five women do you like the best?"

"None."

"That's a first. You not wanting to give me your input."

Jana huffed. "Oh, all right, the last one. At least she's young. The others are old."

"I beg your pardon. Most of them are in their thirties." At least he thought so since he hadn't asked their age. "I'm thirty-six and don't consider myself old."

"How about the first one? No way she's even thirty-nine. Probably more like fifty. Maybe even sixty. She had gray hair. Lots of gray hair."

"There's nothing wrong with gray hair." Touching the side of his head, he'd remembered finding a few gray strands yesterday morning.

"I need someone who can keep up with me. Please not her."

"I'll consider your suggestion. Why did you like the last one?" He recalled Alexa Michaels's pert features. She was pleasing to look at, which wasn't necessarily a good thing.

His wife had been a beauty, and she'd run off with another man. And besides, Ms. Michaels's choice of clothes would keep anyone up at night or at the very least be a beacon in a dark room. And she was too young. He wanted someone with more experience.

Jana shrugged. "Besides not being ancient, she has red hair like me."

"In other words, you don't want anyone."

"Bingo."

He thought of the work piled up on his desk in his office and knew that wasn't going to be an option. He'd been staying up late just to get some of that work done and wasn't sleeping much. That lack was catching up with him.

His daughter wasn't ready to go back to school. She rarely left the yard, and when she did, she was wound so tight he thought she would snap. Going to her therapist's office once a week or on errands with him was about all she could handle and that only lately because of her counseling.

But most of all, the past few months he'd actually enjoyed teaching her. They had grown closer. Jana was doing so much better in her academics from last year. Homeschooling had been good for her. If only he could find someone to keep her on track while he was swamped with work.

He rose. "I'll be in my office. Remember, you have that book to finish reading then write a report on it."

Jana groaned, but flopped into the most comfortable chair in the house in front of the bay window and opened her book. As he left the family room, he glanced back at Jana, an intense look of concentration on her face—a face that reminded him of his ex-wife.

Ian clenched his hands and made his way through the kitchen and living room to his home office. Although folders were stacked high on his desk, the first thing he had to do was call the initial woman he'd interviewed and see if she would take the job. Alexa Michaels wouldn't fit in.

Chapter Two

Finally, the lunch crowd thinned enough that Alexa could take a few moments to rest her weary feet before she headed home. She still wasn't used to standing for long hours. Being a waitress definitely wasn't her preferred job. Besides, she hated the "uniform" they had to wear—a pale blue dress with a white apron and ugly white shoes. She felt as if she was stuck in an old fifties sitcom. All she needed was a little cap on her head.

She eased into a booth with her hot tea and stretched her legs out, flexing her feet. "Ah," she sighed the word and contemplated never getting up. She wished she'd gotten the job with Ian Ferguson, but he'd called last weekend and told her he went with someone else.

She'd thought the Lord had brought her to the Fergusons. She'd only known about the job because Dr. Baker was a friend of his and had insisted he talk with Alexa when Dr. Baker found out he was interviewing others to help him with Jana. Alexa had been wrong, which meant she was stuck with this job unless another one worked out. She had an interview tomorrow, but she just couldn't seem to get excited about it as she had with the Fergusons. There was something about Jana and her situation that pulled at her. The wariness mixed with a touch of sadness made her yearn to help the child. She knew what it was like to lose someone special. At least being a waitress would pay the bills, and she could go to school the spring semester. But her student loans were mounting up. It would be years until she paid them off, and there were so many places she wanted to see.

Taking a sip of her tea, she leaned back and closed her eyes, relishing the rest before she left the café.

Someone cleared his throat. "Ms. Michaels?"

Alexa's eyes flew open to stare up into Ian Ferguson's handsome face—the same face that had plagued a few nights' dreams. For a brief moment, no words came to her mind.

"Are you all right?"

"What are you doing here, Mr. Ferguson?"

He grinned. "I could say I stopped by for lunch."

"It's two-thirty. A little late for lunch. Besides, I'm off the clock now. You'll have to get another waitress."

"I came to see you."

Her heart fluttered, but she squashed that fast. Had he reconsidered about giving her the job? No, it didn't make any difference. There was a reason she didn't get the job. She got the impression they would butt heads over what to do, and he was smart enough to have figured that out. Learning didn't have to happen on a strict schedule, and she wasn't going to change her philosophy because he thought it should. "Why, Mr. Ferguson?"

He slipped into the booth across from her. "Ian, please. My daughter has already reminded me lately I'm old in her eyes. Mr. Ferguson only reinforces that."

"Old? What are you? Forty?"

He grimaced. "Thirty-six." He paused a moment, then leaned toward her. "Are you still interested in the job?"

"Why? What happened to the woman you hired?"

"According to Jana she was Attila the Hun going through menopause. I didn't even know my daughter knew what menopause was."

For a few seconds she suppressed the urge to chuckle, but his perplexed expression coaxed it from her. "You'd be surprised what young girls know today."

"I'm discovering that a lot lately. My little girl is starting to disappear. She'll be eleven in a couple of months, and I'm not ready for her to grow up."

"Before you know it, she'll be a teenager."

"Which really sends a chill through my body."

"Don't let her know. A teen can smell fear and use it to her advantage. It wasn't that long ago that I was one of those creatures." She gave him a smile and a wink.

"Just how old are you?"

"Don't you know that you're not supposed to ask a woman that? Or for that matter, a job applicant," she said in a teasing tone.

He swallowed hard and averted his gaze for a moment, staring across the café as though trying to decide what to say next.

"I'm twenty-three."

"You're right. It hasn't been that long since you were a teen," he said almost to himself.

"Long enough. So what do you want?"

"I'd like to try you out as Jana's nanny/tutor."

Her hand around her cup of tea tightened. "I have a job interview tomorrow with a couple who have three boys. They're friends of the people I worked for as a nanny."

"I understand." Ian leaned back in the booth, but there was nothing relaxing about his ramrod posture.

Alexa folded her arms on the table. "Let's be honest with each other. I got the distinct impression you didn't want me for the job. I think our approaches to life clash." Boy, did they. He was wound too tightly for her. "From what you said, there were others you interviewed. Did you go through the whole list before coming here?"

"No. You're the only other one I asked."

"Why?"

"Because Jana preferred you over the others, especially Attila the Hun. She let me know that this morning, and frankly, after watching my daughter and the woman interact together, I agreed."

"Why did she prefer me? We didn't interact much."

"You're young and have red hair," he said with a grin.

She lifted some strands. "This isn't exactly red."

"What can I say? She's doesn't always think logically or make sense."

Logic would be important to him. Which sent up a red flag. She wasn't known for her logic. Control was important to him also, and long ago she'd given over control to the Lord. Was this His desire? Was that why it hadn't worked out for Attila the Hun? Was that why she hadn't been able to get excited about the other job? "If you don't mind, can I give you an answer tomorrow after my interview?" For a brief moment she was amazed she had said those words as if she would consider working for him rather than the couple she knew. Every logical reason told her to run from him and his job offer.

"Okay."

"And if I decide to work for you, I don't want a trial run. I'll be quitting this job, and I need one that will last."

"It will only last until the end of April."

"That'll be fine. Who knows? You may decide to extend my employment, that is if I take the job."

"Thanks, Ms. Michaels." He slipped from the café's booth.

"Please, I don't usually go by Ms. Michaels. It makes me sound too old." She smiled, remembering his earlier comment. "Call me Alexa, and I'll want Jana to use my first name, too. Will that be a problem?"

He sighed. "No, Alexa. I'll wait for your call before I contact someone else."

As he strode toward the entrance, she prayed the Lord showed her His direction.

"Can I have a word with you, Dr. Baker?" Alexa stuck her head into the office doorway of her adviser at Tall-grass Community College.

"Sure. Come in." Sitting at her desk, the older woman, with short blond hair and a tall, reed-thin body, waved her inside.

Exhausted from tossing and turning the night before, Alexa sank into a chair. "I just had an interview with a couple that offered me a dream job, but when I left the house after talking with Mrs. David, I didn't tell her I would take it. I couldn't say the word *yes.* I kept thinking about Jana Ferguson and what the little girl has been going through with her anxiety." *And what the child's dad was going through.* Behind his austere countenance she'd glimpsed a vulnerability, especially at the café. He seemed lost—grasping to make sense of what was happening to him.

"I thought Ian employed a retired teacher to work with Jana."

"It didn't work out. He's asked me to take over, but I don't think he's totally convinced I'm the right one for the job. I'm not sure I am, either. He wanted to hire me on a trial basis."

"Then take the other one. You need a job." Nancy Baker studied Alexa. "But that's not really what you want to do, is it?"

"No. When I met Jana, I couldn't shake the idea the job was meant for me, but then Ian didn't hire me, so I thought I was wrong. Now I'm not so sure."

"You think the Lord is leading you to the Fergusons?"

"Yes."

"Then you have your answer and everything else will fall into place."

Alexa grasped the arms of her chair and bent forward. "Can you tell me about Jana and her father?"

"I haven't known him for long. We became friends last fall when he started attending Helping Hands Homeschooling meetings for support with teaching his daughter. Ian and I hit it off right away when we discovered he only lived a few blocks from me."

"That's the organization you started for homeschooling parents in this area?"

Nancy nodded. "There was no local support for those parents. I used to get a lot of calls about what they should do for their children. I've never said anything in my classes, but years ago I homeschooled my youngest and struggled at first. There wasn't much around about it then. There is more now, but for these parents in Tallgrass I decided to form the group so they wouldn't go through what I did. It's really grown over the past three years."

The more she got to know Nancy Baker, the more interesting the woman became. She was a widow with two grown sons, and she worked tirelessly for others at the college and their church. And now, Alexa realized, also with Helping Hands Homeschooling. "I'd love to come to one of your meetings. Would that be all right?"

"Sure. Have Ian bring you. He hasn't been able to persuade Jana to attend any of the children's activities we have yet, but he thinks she's close. A couple of times he almost got her to go to the ranch we use for riding lessons. Jana loves animals."

"So you've been around her?"

"Yes, he holds some activities at his house. Last fall we had a fishing rodeo at the lake behind his house, another time a picnic with fun games."

"Do you know what has caused Jana's anxiety?"

"Ian hasn't come out and said anything to me, but it's known that his wife left them. I don't think they have much contact with her. Jana rarely talks about her mother. It's the same with Ian."

"How long has he been a single dad?" She told herself that question was purely for professional reasons, but deep down she couldn't shake a connection that had sprang up between them in his living room. Did it have to do with the young girl or something else? Again the sense he was hurting assailed her, and she was a sucker for wounded people and animals. And when she thought of Jana, she felt the child's pain. Alexa and her father had a troubled relationship. Was that why she felt such a connection with Jana?

"Over a year." Nancy checked her watch. "Oh, dear. I'd better get a move on, or I'll be late for my next class. There's never enough time in the day for all I do." She pushed to her feet and skirted her desk. "Jana's very bright, but last year at school she didn't do well. When she started having similar troubles at the first of this year and giving Ian problems about going to school, he decided to take her out even though all the literature says to try to keep the child with separation anxiety in school if possible. He thought his daughter needed more than what her present situation was offering."

"Do you agree?"

"I'm not the parent. Ian is a smart man who loves his daughter very much. He'll do what's best for Jana. Be warned, I'm not sure Ian will be too easy to deal with at times." She smiled. "But I think you can handle it. I also think this teaching experience will be very rewarding. After this semester, you only have a handful of classes left before your student teaching. You're ready for this."

Am I? "Hard work doesn't scare me." But that brief bond she'd experienced with Ian that day he'd interviewed her did. There were too many things concerning Ian Ferguson that reminded her of her father. Control of any situation had always been so important to her father.

"I know and that's why I think you'd be perfect to shake up their lives." Nancy started for the door with Alexa next to her.

Later, as Alexa left the Education Building on campus, she thought about what her adviser had said. *Shake up their lives? Why does she think they need to be shaken up?*

After parking her repaired car in the driveway on the following Monday, Alexa rang the bell at the Ferguson residence. While she waited, she tapped her booted foot to a country song she'd heard on the way over here. The tune continued to play in her mind.

When the door swung open, she sucked in a deep breath at the disheveled sight of Ian Ferguson standing in the doorway, minus his wire-rimmed glasses, which only highlighted his startlingly blue eyes. His hair was still wet and messy as though he'd just finished towel drying it. He was barefoot but wore black slacks and a gray long-sleeve shirt, hanging out of his pants and buttoned wrong. What stunned her the most, however, was his unsettled expression.

"You're early. Do you always arrive half an hour early?" He combed his fingers through his short hair, trying to bring order to it.

"I didn't want to be late for my first day on the job." She pointed toward her car. "Although fixed, I never know how long the repairs will hold. I've got my cousin on speed dial. Is it okay to leave it parked there?"

"Fine." He stepped to the side to allow her into the house. "Jana's eating breakfast. Why don't you go on into the kitchen and see her. I'll be there in a few minutes."

He padded toward the left, disappearing down a hallway, while she went to the right and immediately spied the girl sitting at an oblong glass table that seated six before a floor-to-ceiling window. As she ate her cereal, listening to her MP3 player, she had a book open on her place mat and was reading it, her forehead wrinkled, a small frown on her face. Jana didn't look up at Alexa until she stopped near the child.

"It's time for school?" Jana's grim expression deepened.

Alexa slipped into the chair near the girl. "No, not yet. I was a little early. I thought the first day we could spend time getting to know each other."

The child's eyes widened. "Have you run that by Dad?"

"Well, no, not yet."

"You'd better. I have a timetable, and I'm sure he's gonna want you to follow it."

A timetable? That sounded worse than a schedule, more rigid. She shouldn't be surprised. But the idea sent a shiver down her length. The years she'd lived at home, her father had insisted she follow a strict schedule—he might as well have said timetable—to the point she'd never felt she could just be a child, spontaneous, perhaps daydreaming, free to let her creative mind come up with something to do. Her mother had been more encouraging of Alexa's naturally carefree nature, but she'd never directly interfered with her husband's mandates.

As soon as she'd graduated from high school, she'd gotten into the used car that her grandfather had given her, and drove until she'd ended up in Tallgrass, Oklahoma, where some of her mother's cousins were. Her father had insisted she go to Vanderbilt University and become a doctor like him. He'd dreamed of his child going into practice with him. When he'd first told her that, she'd laughed, not thinking him serious. She went weak-kneed at the sight of blood. How was she going to be a doctor?

"Okay, I'll have a word with your dad."

"About what?" a deep, gravelly voice said behind her.

Alexa glanced over her shoulder as Ian poured himself some coffee. Not a hair was out of place, and he'd buttoned his shirt correctly, as well as tucked it into his slacks. Didn't he work at home? Or was he going out? "About spending some time with Jana getting to know her before we dig into schoolwork."

"Sure. You have about twenty minutes right now. Would you like some coffee?" He lifted the pot as though preparing to fill a mug for her.

Alexa pressed her lips together before she blurted something out that would get her fired before she'd really started. *Lord, I need patience.* "I'll pass on the coffee. Too bitter for me." She rose, turning completely to face the man. "I was hoping Jana and I could spend a little more time than twenty minutes getting acquainted."

Taking a sip of his drink, he rounded the kitchen island. "How much time are you talking?"

"Personally, I feel it should be all day, but at least this morning."

"All day!" His eyes grew round. He peered beyond

Alexa at his daughter. "Honey, I'm going to give Alexa a tour of the house and show her the room we use for our lessons. Why don't you finish breakfast and read, then come to the classroom in, say—" he glanced at his watch "—thirty minutes."

After a cursory look at the family room off the kitchen, she followed Ian to see the rest of the house, feeling as though she was taking a trip to the principal's office. The tour took five minutes, with him waving his hand toward the entrance into his bedroom from the end of the short hall that led to it. He opened the door to his office and allowed her a quick peek inside—getting the impression of orderliness like an army barracks right before inspection—before moving on. Alexa passed the formal dining room on the way to Jana's bedroom, where he paused for a good minute while she took in the perfectly neat, everything-put-in-a-specific-place room with no posters on the wall and little personal items on display.

The tour finally came to a stop at the classroom—five feet away from Jana's door. He entered and stood off to the side while she circled the row of desks and tried to tamp down her sense of apprehension. This was a sterile model of a classroom in a school except there were only six desks. And why six? Did Jana move from seat to seat with each shift in subject matter?

He waved his hand toward the bookcase. "Those are the textbooks I've been using. I've left detailed notes of what I've covered with Jana and where I stopped." He crossed to the "teacher's desk" and picked up a stack of papers—more like the manuscript of a long book—and gave them to her.

She was in over her head. She didn't care what Nancy Baker thought. This was worse than her adviser realized.

"Since I'll be working a lot, I thought you could turn in

lesson plans each night, and I'll look them over and give them back to you with my notes before you start the next morning. Then you can adjust according to my suggestions."

Examining the very detailed schedule—no, strike that, timetable—of what was to be done down to five- or ten-minute intervals, she really tried to keep the horror from her expression, but she must have failed, because he tilted his head to the side with a puzzled expression and asked, "Is there a problem with that scenario?"

Where do I begin? She drew in a deep, calming breath, then another one. "I know you're paying me to work with Jana and teach her, but I must be able to establish a rapport with her or I won't be able to maximize her learning. Doing that on a timetable is difficult."

"What's wrong with a timetable?"

The genuine inquiry in his question pulled at her. This man didn't realize he didn't control his life. It was in the Lord's hands. No matter how much you structure your life, it could change instantly. Hers had her senior year in high school with the sudden death of her boyfriend. "Nothing per se, and I know that children need structure and boundaries, but not down to every five or ten minutes being planned. Being spontaneous in teaching can keep it exciting and alive for students. Help tap into their curiosity and creativity."

"Jana has been learning much better than the whole of last year."

His defensive tone underscored the fight she would have to change this man's mind. She heaved a sigh and decided to take a risk. "I'm asking you to give me a week my way, and then if I haven't convinced you, I'll try yours."

His eyebrows crunched together. "A week?"

"I need to get to know her. Her likes and dislikes. Her dreams."

"I can tell you those. And although I want you to like Jana, I didn't hire you to be her new best friend. You're the tutor. I'll still be involved some in her education. I promised her I wouldn't totally abandon her."

The force of his voice faded slightly at the end of the last sentence, making Alexa wonder what was behind those words. Was he talking about his wife walking out on the family? Or something else? Again that connection sprang up, and she wanted to help him any way she could with his daughter. He had a way of peering at her in a certain manner that sparked something deep inside her.

He looked away and stared out the window behind the teacher's desk. Finally, after a long minute, he swung his full attention back to her. "Tell you what. I'll give you a day to get to know my daughter. Then you can follow my schedule."

She should make a stand and walk if he didn't agree to her terms. She stared at the stony expression on his face now as though he regretted that brief glimpse of vulnerability. For that full minute she'd seen a war of emotions—pain, sadness, anger—flicker in and out of his eyes, and it had touched her more than she wanted to acknowledge. He wasn't as in control of his emotions as he desired. Suddenly leaving Jana, and even Ian, was distasteful to Alexa. She would make this work somehow.

Lord, I'm gonna need Your help BIG time.

"Fine. I'll take your schedule home tonight and study it." *Since I can't burn it.* "And I appreciate the notes on where Jana is educationally." She gave him a sweet smile, remembering the look of hurt and sadness she'd seen in his eyes.

"I'm glad we're finally on the same page."

Of different books. Alexa headed for the hallway, needing to get out of the sterile classroom with a bookcase, one teacher desk and six student desks, a dry eraser board, a state-of-the-art computer and printer and a world globe. Her first job would be getting to know the ten-year-old child in her charge. The second was doing something about that classroom if she had to stay and teach in it. It needed color, posters, items to excite a child to learn.

In the corridor Alexa shifted to face him. "Why six desks?"

"If you look over the schedule, you'll see where a group of students come to the house for math. I participate in a co-op through Helping Hands Homeschooling."

"They do? Does Jana go to their house for classes?" Although she was pretty sure of the answer after talking with Nancy Baker, she hoped to get more information from Ian about their situation.

"Not yet. We do some things here, and it gets her around other children her age."

"You told me she doesn't go to a lot of places," she said, trying another tactic to get some answers to the multiple questions she had about what had happened to make Jana the way she was. What happened to put that look of sadness in her eyes?

"She'll go to the therapist and has managed a couple of other places with me there. But so far, that's all." His expression closed down, a tic twitching in his jawline.

"How about around the neighborhood, lake, yard?"

"Definitely the lake by our house and our yard. She's also gone to our next-door neighbors'. Kelly babysits her some, always here, however. Alexa will go see Kelly sometimes, but never for long."

"Kelly lives next door?"

"Yes, on the right. She's fifteen and has befriended my daughter." In the kitchen he refilled his mug with coffee. "I'll be in my office if you need anything. We eat lunch at eleven-thirty."

"Okay," Alexa murmured while he left.

She definitely would go home tonight and read up on separation anxiety, but she didn't need to be a rocket scientist to figure out Jana was scared her father would leave her as her mother had. Alexa knew about loss. She also knew what it was like to be estranged from a parent. Although her father was marginally in her life, their relationship was shaky at best. What few conversations on the phone they'd had in the past five years had been stilted and formal. The pain of his rejection still twisted her stomach in a huge knot.

Entering the kitchen, Alexa covered the distance to Jana and sat next to her. When the child removed her earplugs and peered at her, Alexa asked, "What are you reading?"

"*Silas Marner*," Jana said as though she'd taken a dose of foul-tasting medicine.

Nancy had said Jana was bright, and Alexa was beginning to see how bright. "What do you think of the story?"

"Booor—ing."

"Then don't read it. There are tons of good stories out there for you to enjoy."

"Dad wants me to read one classic a week. I love to read, just not these type." She flipped her hand toward the book. "They're slow. I don't care about the past."

"Like any book, if you don't care for the topic, it won't be as interesting to you." She pointed to the paperback. "For today I'd like you to put it aside. You can finish it tomorrow."

"But Dad was gonna talk to me at dinner tonight about it."

"I'm sure he can postpone it until tomorrow evening." At least she hoped he would amend his schedule this one time. "He thought we should get to know each other first."

Doubt turned the corners of Jana's mouth down. "He did?" Jana scraped her chair back and leaped to her feet then whirled around and charged across the kitchen into the hallway.

Alexa quickly followed, hoping the path to Ian's office didn't become worn by the end of the day.

Jana hurried in to see her father. "Dad, I thought I had to finish *Silas Marner* this morning and write a report. Have you changed your mind? She says I don't have to do it today."

Alexa appeared in the doorway, the challenge to her authority still ringing in her ears. Ian's narrowed gaze fixed on her. He'd begrudgingly gone along with the plan for her to get to know Jana first. Would he openly challenge her in front of his daughter?

Chapter Three

As Ian took in the pair standing in his office, his attention shifted from Alexa to his daughter. "Honey, you and Alexa will be spending a lot of time together. I think it would be nice if you two got to know each other." He closed the file on the computer he was working on, preparing for Jana's protest.

"What about the book?" Jana asked with a huff.

"We'll talk about it tomorrow evening." *Tonight I'm going to be questioning you about Alexa. Did I make the right decision?* There had been another candidate he'd interviewed who might have worked out. She was younger than the first one and had worked as a teacher's assistant in another state. But for some reason he couldn't even define, he'd decided to go with Jana's reluctant choice out of all the candidates. Had his daughter changed her mind already? That was quicker than the Attila the Hun debacle.

"Fine." Jana flounced out of the office, passing Alexa, who stepped to the side.

After Jana left, Alexa stayed, even moving a few more paces into the room. "Thank you. You won't regret hiring me."

"I hope you're right. My daughter's welfare means everything to me." *She's all I have, and I won't ever abandon her like her mother did.*

Alexa flashed him a smile, "I can see that," then swung around and walked from the office.

He could read her every emotion on her face, and he knew she was wary of him. She thought he was too rigid in his ways. That hadn't always been the case. Once he'd embraced life as it had come at him until one incident after another had knocked any spontaneity from him.

Alexa reminded him of what it felt like to be impulsive… and happy. The thought sent panic through him. She was so different from people he gravitated toward. She was too much like his ex-wife—flamboyant, carefree, too flexible. And even worse, Alexa and he were years apart. At least he and Tracy were close to the same age.

Although he and his wife had had problems in their marriage, he'd thought they could work them out. She hadn't. Her walking away without a backward glance had sucker punched him. He'd desperately tried to cling to something and found that a schedule and structure in his life, as well as Jana's, had helped even more than before. Going with the flow only caused a person to go aimlessly through life with no purpose.

He'd give Alexa today. Tomorrow was his.

"This is a beautifully carved bench. I can't believe your father made it." Not sure if she should sit on the piece of furniture that was more a work of art than anything else, Alexa ran her hand over the intricately patterned design in the wood, which had begun to weather. She couldn't believe it sat under a large oak tree where the elements could rain down on it. Hours had been spent on this piece, and it seemed as though it had been carelessly tossed outside to deteriorate.

"Yeah, Dad used to do woodworking a lot, mostly on the weekends." Jana tossed a pebble into the lake then plopped down on the bench. "This was his last piece."

Alexa took the seat next to the child. "Used to? He doesn't anymore?"

"No, he stopped when—" Jana snapped her mouth close. Her jawline firmed into a clenched countenance.

As much as Alexa wished she and Jana could talk about her mother, Alexa kept those questions locked away for another time. "That's a shame. He's very good."

"Yeah." Jana spread her legs apart and dangled her clasped hands between them. "He'd been in the middle of making me a bench for my room. He never finished it. It's still sitting in the garage half done."

"Did you ask him about it?"

"No. Things just haven't been the same—lately."

"Where did he work? The garage?"

"Yeah. Since it had been built for three cars, he used the extra space to make a small workshop for himself so he could get as messy as he wanted."

Messy? Ian? From all she'd seen, she hadn't thought him capable. Well, maybe except for the stack of files on his desk in his office. But even they had been in an orderly pile. Then she remembered his tousled hair and his shirt buttoned wrong, as if he'd hurried when she'd arrived this morning. Her breath caught as the picture materialized in her mind. She quickly shook that image away and asked, "Did you ever make anything with wood?"

"Nope. That doesn't interest me."

"What does, besides reading good books?" Although she'd discovered a few things about Jana today, the child had been pretty closemouthed most of the morning. She'd ended up telling the young girl about herself, hoping to make some kind of connection.

"I love animals." Jana pointed out on the lake. "See those geese and ducks? It won't be too much longer before they'll have babies. When that happens, I keep a running tally of how many. Last year we had forty-three babies born here."

"What's your favorite animal?"

"Dogs. I never got to have one."

"I have a dog named Charlie. I got him a few years back at the pound. He's been the best pet and a great watchdog except that when anyone new comes into my house he runs and hides. Barks like crazy while they're outside, though." Alexa watched several Canada geese circle the lake then glide down until they lit upon the water. "What's stopping you from having a pet?"

Jana didn't say anything for a long moment, her hands twisting together. Her expression darkened, her eyebrows slashing downward. Was this something to do with her mother? Had the woman disliked animals?

"Jana, are you all right?"

"I kept thinking Mom would return home. She's allergic to dogs and I didn't want to have to get rid of a pet. I guess she isn't gonna." Her pout increased. "She doesn't even call. She's written a couple of times, but I want to talk to her. I even tried calling her once. No one answered. The second time I called the same number it was disconnected." Jana drew in a shaky breath.

Alexa waited a few minutes to see if Jana would elaborate. When she didn't, Alexa said, "I know when I've had a particularly bad day I love hugging and petting Charlie. He's the best pick-me-upper."

Jana shook her head, as though ridding her thoughts of something unpleasant, and focused on Alexa. "What kind is he?"

"Oh, a mix of four or five kinds probably. He's large, black and brown with a little white around the face. He has a long tail that wags constantly unless he's running and hiding."

Jana laughed.

The lilting sound was beautiful, the first time Alexa had heard it. The child lounged back, her long legs stretched out.

"I hope you'll bring Charlie over one day. I'd love to meet him."

"I'm not sure your dad would like to have Charlie in the house. He can get overenthusiastic and bump into things. I've lost a few items because he's crashed into them. But anytime you want to visit him at my house, I'd love to have you."

Jana's relaxed expression dissolved. "Maybe," she murmured, although she didn't sound very convincing. Straightening, she glanced at her watch. "It's eleven-thirty. Lunch will be ready." She hopped to her feet and hurried toward the covered patio.

A ten-year-old wearing a watch? Alexa shook her head. A child shouldn't be that concerned about time yet. That was one piece of jewelry she didn't own—wouldn't.

Alexa covered the distance to the patio and entered the kitchen to find Jana standing in the middle of it, her face pale, her whole body shaking. "What's wrong?"

"Dad's not here! He should be here." Tears streamed down her cheeks.

"Have you checked his office?" Alexa hurried toward the girl and wrapped her arms around her, half expecting Jana to pull away.

But she didn't. She buried herself against Alexa. "Yes. He always has lunch ready by this time. Something's happened."

She stroked her hand down the child's back. "I'm sure he's fine. He probably had to run an errand. I can fix us something to eat."

"No, he tells me when he's leaving." A sob escaped Jana's mouth, then another.

Alexa hugged the girl, wishing she could erase the anxiety that gripped Jana. The sound of her crying riveted her full attention until Alexa heard the garage door going up. She eased back and looked into the child's tear-streaked face. "Your dad is home."

Swiping her cheeks, Jana flew from Alexa's arms and raced toward the door to the garage, flinging it open. As Alexa came to the entrance, the girl hurled herself into her father's embrace.

"Where were you? You scared me. I thought something had happened to you." Jana's breathless words tumbled from her mouth.

"Honey, I'm so sorry. I thought I would go grab us all some burgers. I wasn't going to be gone long, but got caught in a construction zone. I tried calling. No one answered. I figured you were still outside." Ian peered at Alexa, pain in his eyes. "I didn't mean to scare you. You and Alexa were busy talking and…" The rest of his explanation faded into the silence— a silence only broken by Jana's renewed sobbing.

Alexa approached the pair. "Let me take the burgers and get the table set." She felt as though she'd stepped into the middle of a family moment she had no business witnessing.

"Thanks." Ian held out the paper bag, the scent of fries peppering the air.

Over the top of his daughter's head, his gaze linked with hers. With his brow creased, his vulnerability reached out to Alexa, making her want to smooth his worries away. She hurriedly snatched the bag and rushed inside.

She'd been there herself five years before when her high school sweetheart was killed in a freak accident on a baseball field. Her whole life had been rocked to its foundation, changed in one instant. They'd planned to marry the following year after graduation even though her father would have objected and tried to stop the wedding. It wouldn't have made any difference. She'd loved Daniel and what they'd shared hadn't been puppy love as her father had told her several times. Although Daniel hadn't walked out on her, he'd left her to face her father alone and to pick up the pieces of her life.

Her hands trembling, Alexa set the food down on a place mat, clasping the edge of the table for a few seconds before she went to the refrigerator and withdrew a pitcher of ice water and a carton of milk. After retrieving some glasses from the cabinet, she sat to wait for Ian and Jana and try to make some sense out of why she was led to them. The sound of the door to the garage opening drew her attention. Her young charge, her eyes red but the fear gone from her expression, hurried into the kitchen, making a beeline for the chair she'd used that morning, and plopped into it.

"I love the food from Incredible Burger." Jana squirted ketchup on her plate and scooped some up with a fry, then popped it into her mouth.

"I know. That's why I thought I'd go get some hamburgers instead of fixing sandwiches," a sober Ian said, striding toward them.

"I have to agree with Jana. Incredible Burger has the best food." Alexa took a bite of her thick, juicy hamburger. "Jana told me you used to do woodworking. I was admiring that bench you made. It's beautiful."

Ian's gaze strayed toward the window that overlooked the backyard. "That was one of my best pieces."

"Do you have any others around here?"

"No, I've given them away. Most of them were smaller. I hadn't been doing carpentry that long, and now I don't have the time."

He might not realize the wistfulness that sounded in his voice when he said that last sentence, but Alexa heard it. Everyone needed a creative outlet. She suspected that Ian's had been his woodwork pieces.

"Dad, I've got one of your boxes."

"I forgot about that. It was one of my first attempts."

"I love it. I keep my treasures in it."

Alexa took a sip of her ice water. "May I see it?"

"Yeah, I'll get it." Jana started to get up.

"Pumpkin, you can wait until after lunch."

The child dropped back onto her chair. "Alexa told me she has a dog named Charlie. She got him at the pound. Can we get a dog from the pound?"

"What about the geese and ducks that like to wander into our yard?"

"We can get a small dog that stays in the house. When it needs to go out, I'll walk it on a leash."

Ian's gaze swept to Alexa for a long moment, his doubt that a pet would be a good fit for Jana and him in his expression. When he peered at his daughter, he said, "A dog will cause prob—" His words sputtered to a stop. "If you want a dog from the pound, you'll have to go and pick it out. A pet's a very personal decision, not one I'll do for you."

"I can get an animal." Excitement filled Jana's voice, and a smile encompassed her whole face for half a minute until she paused, her forehead wrinkled. Her mouth scrunched up into a frown. "We'd go together?"

"Of course."

"I'll think about it." Jana dived into the rest of her

lunch, silent, staring at the place mat as though mulling over her dilemma.

At the end of the meal Ian stood and gathered up the trash. "Jana, I have an appointment this afternoon at two. I'll be back by three-thirty. Okay?"

His daughter locked gazes with him and nodded, then picked up the three empty glasses and took them to the sink. "I'm gonna get the box."

When they were alone, Ian paused near Alexa, throwing a glance toward the doorway Jana left through. "I imagine you have questions. Is it possible for you to stay this evening for dinner and then you and I can talk afterward?"

"What are you going to have?"

"For dinner?"

"Yes."

"What if I said I don't know?" A twinkle gleamed in his eyes, his dimple winking at her.

"I wouldn't believe you. You're the type who has his meals all planned for the week, possibly even the whole month."

"I was spontaneous today with lunch, and look what happened."

"And everything is okay now."

"Spaghetti. And I only plan one week at a time."

"I thought you didn't cook much."

"From a jar," he said sheepishly.

"I'll stay on one condition. I cook dinner with Jana's help."

"She doesn't cook, either."

"She needs to learn. *Everyone* needs to fend for themselves."

He splayed his hand over his heart. "Ouch."

"Don't get me wrong. I've cut corners in cooking a meal, too. We all do. But I can use this to teach Jana. Although I know my spaghetti recipe by heart, I'll write it down and show her how to follow it. Not to mention she'll have to do different measurements. I can make enough so you two have leftovers. That means doubling the amounts. You said math isn't her strong area. This'll be a fun way to do some."

"I don't have the ingredients."

"I wish she would go with me to the grocery, but I know we aren't there yet. How about you get what I need on the way home from your appointment? Or I can go after you get back."

"I'll let you get the supplies. Madge does most of my grocery shopping. That's why I plan my meals for the week." A defensive tone entered his voice.

"There's nothing wrong with planning what you're gonna eat. Even I do that."

"You do? I got the impression you didn't plan a thing."

"It's hard not to do some. I just try not to get tied down by it." She glanced toward Jana reentering the kitchen. "You and I are fixing dinner tonight."

The child's eyes grew round. "Why?"

"Because your dad invited me to eat with you two, and I don't do spaghetti out of a jar."

Jana looked from Alexa to her father then burst out laughing. "Finally, someone who feels like I do."

"Where did you learn to cook so well?" Ian asked as he stepped out onto the porch with Alexa that evening. "That was the best spaghetti I've ever had."

"Your daughter had a hand in making it, too."

"When I came through the kitchen, it seemed like you were doing an awful lot of instructing and demonstrating and my daughter was doing an awful lot of listening."

As she walked toward her car in the driveway, she slowed

and shifted toward Ian, the glow from the porch light illuminating his face, none of the tension earlier at lunch visible. "And she was learning. She had no problem doubling the recipe for me. We talked about equivalents and measurements. She may be weak in math, but she did great."

He started forward. "I sometimes worry she avoids math because that's my strong subject. She's bright in so many other things like reading and writing."

"Math can be so logical and analytical. English appeals to a person's creativity. Math is full of rules, and yes, there are rules in grammar, but they're more fluid than when you deal with numbers. Two plus two is always four."

At her car he lounged back against it, folding his arms over his chest. "Thanks for staying and cooking dinner. A guy could get used to that. I liked your suggestion of Jana reading *White Fang*. When she heard it was about a wolf, did you see her eyes light up?"

"I hope she'll get a dog."

"Another thing I owe to you. I haven't talked to my daughter about getting a pet since before my wife left. But I think it would be good for Jana, especially now she needs something to focus her attention on. I know pets can be good company." He heaved a deep breath. "Which brings me to one of the reasons I wanted to talk with you in private without a young girl listening in. I've decided I'll let you do things your way, and I'll see how it works out."

Her mouth dropped open, and she sank against the side of her car next to Ian, her arm for just a second brushing against him. She immediately put a few inches between them and tried to dismiss the jolt from the brief contact.

"No written lesson plans every evening?" She'd never thought it would be that easy to get him to change his mind. Was he more flexible than she'd originally thought?

"Not exactly, but I do want to know what you're doing. Maybe we can touch base in the morning and then before you leave. And I'll still be doing the twice-a-week math lesson with the other students. I'm hoping between those lessons you can help Jana get a better handle on what I've presented."

His musk-scented aftershave lotion teased her senses, causing a parade of images of him throughout the day to flow through her mind. Ian smiling at her from across the table. Ian laughing at one of her stories about working with children at an elementary school. Ian caring about his daughter and not afraid to show her. She needed to stop her train of thought concerning this man who had been wounded by his wife. She would only be here temporarily. They were from two very different worlds, years apart in age. "When do you have the others here for math?" she asked when she realized the silence had lasted over a minute and Ian was staring at her.

"Every Wednesday and Friday afternoon from three to four."

"And is the other reason you wanted to talk with me about what happened right before lunch?"

Ian stiffened and pushed off the car, rotating toward her. "Yes. When Jana feels insecure, she freaks out. If she thinks I'm supposed to be someplace and I'm not, she doesn't handle that very well. She's much better than she was. Her therapist is doing a great job with her."

"I know it's none of my business, but what happened with her mother? Maybe if I understand, I can help in some way." She wouldn't be surprised if he told her to butt out, but she had to ask. She would be with the child most days for the next four months.

Ian kneaded his nape, peering off into space. The

sound of a dog barking broke the silence that had descended between them. He stabbed her with a piercing look. "This isn't something I usually talk about, but you have a point." His hand rubbed even harder at the muscles in his neck.

His tension flowed from him and enclosed about her. The urge to soothe his hurt inundated her.

"The only good part of the story is that my ex-wife, Tracy, left us on a day Madge worked, so when Jana came home from school, someone was here to let her in. Tracy left a message on my cell phone that she was leaving us. I had my office downtown then. I didn't get the message until late, right before Madge was to go home. Jana was worried, pacing the living room. She didn't understand where her mom was. They were supposed to go shopping after school for a project Jana had. Worried, Madge called my secretary. That's when I went and checked my cell, then left work and came right home. That's the first clue I had that my wife was having an affair. She ran off with a man she met online and had been secretly seeing the past few months."

"So Jana's afraid you'll abandon her like her mother did?"

"That's obvious and something we're working through. We're to the point where I don't have to be in the therapist's office with Jana for her sessions, and I can leave to run errands as long as she knows exactly where and when I'm going. She'll stay with Madge or Kelly and now you. I made the mistake of not coming out to tell Jana I'd decided to go get burgers. I should have been gone only fifteen minutes. Instead, it was more like thirty."

"She finished school last year. How?"

"Not easily. She wasn't doing great before her mother left. But afterward, her grades plummeted. Then summer came, and she got even clingier. Finally I quit my job and opened my own office here at home. I've cut back on my workload in order to be here for Jana."

"How long has she been in therapy?"

"Since the end of June, when I saw how difficult everything was becoming for Jana. I think she tried to hold it together and did for a while. In my confusion and the mess I was dealing with, I didn't see how bad her struggle was. But finally she couldn't keep up her front, and she went rapidly downhill. I'm having a hard time forgiving myself for that."

Although she couldn't see his expression well in the dim lighting, frustration, pain and a touch of bewilderment marked his voice. All she wanted to do was comfort. She reached out and laid her hand on his arm. He peered down at her fingers on him then up into her face. The bond between them, as though they both understood what it was like to be abandoned by a loved one, strengthened.

"Knowing how much you care for Jana, I'm sure you were doing the best you could."

He pulled his arm away, breaking the bond. "No, I wasn't. I was licking my wounds. But I've learned one valuable lesson from what happened with Tracy. I won't let something like that happen to me or to my daughter again. I will protect my daughter at all costs. Good night, Alexa." He turned away and began striding toward the porch. "I'll see you tomorrow."

Not only would he protect Jana at all costs, but she was sure he wanted to protect himself, too. Although she didn't see his shoulders slump, she sensed he'd felt weighted down. He was struggling with his emotions concerning his ex-wife's abandonment of Jana, but also of himself. Anger bound him up in impotency as if he were running as fast as he could and not going anywhere.

His expression reminded her of how she'd felt when her

father had told her if she walked out of his house never to come back. After that their relationship had never been the same. She wouldn't follow in her father's footsteps, and he wouldn't accept that from her. The memory threatened her composure, prodding her anger forward.

How can someone turn away from his family? Is this the way Ian felt concerning his wife leaving him and Jana? Is the reason I'm here to help him through the pain of his loss? To help him forgive his wife? I'm not sure I can, Lord. I don't know if I can ever forgive my father, so how can I show someone else how? God would reveal his reasons in time. For once she would have to practice patience and wait.

Alexa slid into her front seat and backed out of the driveway. Her first day on the job had wiped her out emotionally and physically. And yet she would go back tomorrow and put everything she had into her work because the Lord had placed the Ferguson family in her life for a reason.

As she pulled into the driveway to her duplex, she noted a car parked on the street in front of her place. When she climbed from her vehicle, someone got out of the one by the curb. A tall woman. She pivoted toward Alexa, the streetlight catching her face in its brilliance. Alexa gasped.

"Mom! What are you doing here? You aren't suppose to visit me until spring break." Every year her mother came to Tallgrass for a week to see her. Her father never accompanied her, and Alexa didn't want to strain what little relationship her father and she had by going home.

"Your dad and I had a fight. I've left him."

Chapter Four

Half an hour later, after letting Charlie out into the yard and getting herself settled, Alexa sat with her mother at the kitchen table, cradling a cup of herbal tea between her hands. She hoped for its soothing effects to work quickly. She couldn't believe what her mom had said to her out in the street.

"What happened?" Alexa took a long sip of her warm drink. "You two have been married for twenty-five years."

"I told him I wanted to go back to work." Gloria's voice quavered with each word she uttered.

"As a nurse?"

"Yes. After he went through medical school and internship, your father didn't want me to work. Ever since you graduated from high school, I've needed more." As her mother lifted her mug to her lips, her hand trembled. "I've sat by for years letting him run my life. I think it's about time I do it myself. I told him I was coming to visit you and staying until he came to his senses."

"So you're not really leaving him?"

"It depends on him. This has been brewing for years. I

need some breathing room. I need to decide what I want to do—not what your father wants me to do."

Alexa swept her arm to indicate her small kitchen off her small living room. "This isn't a large place."

"It's a cute duplex and you have two bedrooms. I don't need a lot of space. I have some money and can help you with expenses. I can get a job here. Nurses are in demand."

Mixed feelings swamped Alexa. She was happy her mother was here visiting, but not the way it had occurred. She understood what her mother was feeling. Finally, her mom had stood up to her dad. But she hated to see their marriage come apart. Alexa had rebelled against her father's wishes, and now they barely spoke. She would talk to her mother while she was staying with her and see if she could help. If Alexa had to, she'd try calling her father and talking to him, even though she doubted he would listen to her.

"Mom, I work all day, and starting next week, I'll be going to school Tuesday and Thursday evenings. You might get lonely being by yourself so much."

"While I was waiting for you, I met your neighbor in the other duplex. She's a lovely woman. I can also get involved at your church and start looking for that job. And don't forget, my cousins live here. You don't need to worry about me." Gloria patted Alexa's arm. "Tell me about your new job."

Her mom had always been good at diverting her attention from the problem at hand, and this was no different. "I'm tutoring a young girl who's ten. She is homeschooled by her father, except this is tax season and he's a CPA. He needed help for the next four months."

"Where's his wife?"

"He's divorced. She isn't in the picture. I'm not even sure he knows where she is."

"Why doesn't the little girl go to school?"

"Her mother leaving them has been especially hard on her. Ian says she's doing so much better this year than last, when she was at school."

"You know, when you were in elementary school I thought about homeschooling you, but I decided it wasn't for me, and your father was against it. It's much more accepted now than it was back then."

Alexa tried to remember any incident where her mother had done what she'd felt she should rather than following her husband's dictates. She couldn't. Why now? Midlife crisis? "How did Dad feel about you coming to see me every spring break? Why didn't he ever come?"

"You know how stubborn he can be."

"You mean he's really still upset over me not doing what he wanted—becoming a doctor?"

"Yeah, he thinks you are wasting your life, but I wasn't going to let his attitude stop me from seeing you." She rose, skirted the table and drew Alexa up. "Hon, nothing should come between a mother and her child. Nothing." She gave Alexa a hug that she cherished because over the past five years she'd had so few of them.

"Then how could Ian's wife leave Jana and not have contact with her?" Alexa asked when she pulled back. Did the woman know the damage she had caused?

"I can't answer that. Only she can." Her mother cupped her face. "Maybe you'll be able to help Jana."

"Mom, thanks for bringing Charlie." On Ian's front porch Thursday, Alexa stooped to pat her dog. "Let me get Jana. She's so excited to meet Charlie."

Alexa hurried back into the foyer and ran right into Ian coming out of his office.

He steadied her. "I thought I heard the doorbell."

His hands still on her arms, Alexa scrambled to come up with a reply. His nearness threw her equilibrium off. When he released her and stepped back, she breathed again and said, "You did. My mother's here with my dog. Jana wanted to see him. We were researching different dog breeds, and Jana thought it would be fun to try to figure out what breeds Charlie has in him. Jana is trying to decide what kind of dog she wants."

"Your mom's in Tallgrass? Didn't you say something to my daughter about your parents living in Kentucky?"

"Yeah. Mom's been here since Monday. She's on the porch."

Ian started toward the front door. "I'll invite—"

"Don't." She reached to stop him and realized what she was doing. She kept her arm at her side. "Remember, Charlie's a handful, especially in a strange place. I think it'll be best if Jana goes outside to see him."

Chuckling, he swung around. "It's a few days since we talked about getting a pet from the pound, but she keeps changing her mind about what she wants. Maybe this will help her. I'm hoping she'll just go to the pound with me and pick one out."

Alexa stepped back a few paces, needing some more space between them. "I'll encourage her to, if that's okay with you."

"Better yet. I can take a break in a while, and we can all go together to the pound. That might spur her decision."

"That would be great." She backed away several more steps and nearly collided with a table along one wall of the foyer. "Give us a few minutes, and Mom and I will be on the patio with Charlie."

"I'll get Jana and meet you out back, then."

As she made her way to her mother, she thought of the

past four days working for Ian and teaching Jana. He'd been so busy she'd hardly seen him, which had been fine by her. When she was around him, she found it hard to concentrate on what she should be doing. His presence flustered her, especially if he stopped by where Jana and she were working.

Out on the porch Alexa took Charlie's leash from her mother and started for the side of the house. "Ian and Jana are coming out on the patio."

"You haven't said too much about the man you're working for."

"There isn't much to say, Mom." She hoped her mother would drop the subject. Gloria Michaels could be a pit bull when she set her mind on something, and frankly Alexa was trying to sort out the mixed feelings Ian generated in her.

"Your dad called me this morning after you left for work."

Alexa slowed her step and glanced at her mother. "And?"

"He asked me one question. Have I come to my senses yet? I told him no, and that was the end of the conversation."

Alexa clenched her teeth, trying her best not to say anything to her mother. Once she'd wanted to get married, until her boyfriend had been suddenly taken from her. Now she couldn't see herself marrying. Her parents' marriage hadn't been a great model for her. If wedded bliss was like that, she wanted no part of it. "I'm sorry," she said finally.

Her mother slipped her arm around Alexa's shoulder. "Don't worry. I'm enjoying myself here. Your neighbor and I are going to lunch today. I told you not to be concerned about me."

"I won't," she murmured, but knew she would. Although she and her father didn't see eye to eye on a lot of things, she didn't want to see her parents' marriage dissolve.

Charlie picked up speed, practically dragging Alexa

around the corner to the backyard. He saw Jana on the patio and made a beeline for her, his tail wagging and hitting Alexa in the leg. She tightened her grip on the leash.

"Jana and Ian, this is Charlie, and this—" Alexa pointed to her mother "—is Gloria Michaels, my mom. She's visiting me for a while."

Ian shook Gloria's hand while Jana said hi, then turned her smile on the dog.

The young girl knelt and threw her arms around Charlie, letting him lick her face. Jana's giggles reverberated through the warm January morning. "He's great, Alexa." When the child stood, she asked, "Can I take him for a walk by the lake?"

"Sure." Alexa gave her the leash. "Hold him tight or he might go after the geese or ducks. If he gets too hard to handle, drop the leash and let me know."

"I will."

"When you said he was big, you meant it. Maybe I should walk with her." Ian took a step toward his daughter.

"Charlie loves people. She'll be all right. If he gets away, he'll come to my whistle."

Gloria stepped in to the conversation. "My daughter tells me you are a CPA working from your home. How do you like having a home office?"

Ian shifted toward her mother, his glance straying toward Jana occasionally. "I didn't think I would, but I'm actually enjoying it."

Gloria Michaels's gaze roamed down his length. "Yeah, you don't have to worry about wearing a business suit. You can work in sweats. Be casual. Are you going out to a meeting?"

Ian peered down at his dark navy pants and light blue long-sleeved, button-down shirt. "No."

"Oh, I just thought…" Her mother's voice faded into the silence, a flush to her cheeks. She swept around to watch Jana coming back from the edge of the lake.

Alexa pressed her lips together to keep from smiling at the discomfort crossing Ian's face. He dressed up more to go to his office in his home than she did to go to church.

Jana stopped a few feet away, kneeling next to Charlie. "I think he's part German shepherd, part collie, maybe some Great Dane. What do ya think?"

Ian circled the large dog, rubbing his chin. "I definitely think part Great Dane. Now I understand why Alexa doesn't want to bring him inside."

"I've decided I want a big dog—like Charlie."

Frowning, Ian faced his daughter. "No. We agreed upon a small one."

Alexa could see the horror that flitted across Ian's expression, as though he'd just pictured Charlie running wild through his house, crashing into one thing after another. Which was definitely possible with a dog like Charlie.

"But, Dad—"

"We've never had a pet. Let's start small and see how things go."

"But Alexa lives in a duplex and Charlie does fine." Jana's pout descended.

Alexa started to tell Jana that she didn't have that much furniture in her place and not much of value to destroy, as well as a fenced backyard, but her mother stepped toward the young girl.

"I can bring Charlie back another day for a visit if you all want, but I have a lunch date and need to get Charlie home." Her mom took the leash from the child. "It was nice meeting you two."

Before Gloria left, Jana bent over and hugged the dog,

burying her face against the side of his neck. "Bye, boy. Maybe you can come back again for a longer visit."

Alexa sidled next to Ian and whispered, "She may fall in love with a small dog at the pound."

"Let's hope."

After her mother and Charlie left, Jana swiveled toward her father. "Let's go to the pound now."

Ian checked his watch. "Fine. Then we can grab something to eat on the way home."

"In a restaurant?" A tinge of panic laced Jana's voice.

"We can use the drive-through or go inside the burger place. It'll be your call, Jana."

"We can't leave a dog in the car. We'll have to use the drive-through."

"You're right. I hadn't thought of that." Ian started for the house. "I'm going to have to adjust my thinking with a dog around."

"Actually—" Alexa glanced back at the young girl still standing at the edge of the patio "—Jana, you won't be able to bring your dog home until tomorrow. A vet will need to check it over first."

"I have to wait." The corners of Jana's mouth inched down.

"That'll give you time to get everything you need, like food, bedding, maybe a few toys." Alexa paused walking when Ian did.

"Yeah," Jana's expression brightened. "After we eat, we can go to the pet store and buy what we need."

Surprise flashed into Ian's eyes. "You want to go to the store?"

"The deal we had was I had to take care of my pet, so I should pick out its bedding and toys." Jana raced toward the back door.

"Are you ready for this?" Alexa hung back with Ian.

"Sure, how hard can it be? We'll get a little dog. How much damage can a little one do?"

She wasn't going to tell him about the first dog she got when she was a teenager that her father gave away because it chewed everything it could get hold of, including his favorite pair of dress shoes.

Jana stood at one end of the rows of cages at the pound, her forehead creased, her mouth twisted in a perplexed expression. "How can I pick just one?"

"Because you have to." The thought of more than one pet running around his house caused Ian's gut to roil.

His daughter trudged down the middle of the long narrow room, surveying each animal as she passed. Pausing in front of one, she pointed at the dog. "He's cute. He kinda looks like Charlie, Alexa. Whatcha think?"

Alexa came to view the huge dog with its nose pressed against the cage.

Ian heard "looks like Charlie" and his stomach churned even more. He should have insisted on picking out the pet and bringing it home for Jana. Knowing Jana's love for animals, he was sure she would have fallen in love with any dog he'd brought home. "You can pick any dog fifteen inches or shorter."

"Any one?" Jana moved on to the next potential pet. "Can I get a dog a little bigger?"

Ian released a long breath. "Maybe an inch or so."

At the end of the row, Jana knelt in front of a cage and tilted her head from one side to the other as she studied the animal inside. "Mmm, Alexa, what breeds do you think this one has in him?"

"Maybe we should eliminate what breeds he doesn't have."

"Well, he's not a Great Dane or German shepherd," Jana replied, ticking off large breeds.

His kind of dog. Small. Easier to handle. Ian covered the distance between Jana and him and peered inside at the animal. The ugliest dog he'd ever seen stood, wagging its tail, panting. Well, at least it fit his height requirement.

"Isn't he cute?" Jana asked him.

The "cute" dog jumped up, putting its huge front paws on the wire cage. "It's a she," was all Ian could think of to say.

"I think I'll name her Sugar."

Alexa bent down next to Jana and patted the animal through the bars. "She's adorable."

What? Are you two blind? He kept that opinion to himself. At least the dog was small, even if it was oblong like a dachshund and hairless, not to mention having squatty bowlegs like a bulldog, a tight curly tail like a pig and sagging jowls like a bloodhound. "Have you looked at the ones in this row?" He took a step toward the cages on the other side.

Jana stayed put. "I want her."

"Are you sure?"

His daughter nodded.

Okay, this would be all right. So the dog was ugly. She appeared to be affectionate and probably would be grateful to have a home. "Then let's tell them."

He left Alexa and Jana and went in search of the attendant who was just on the other side of the door. "We want the dog in number twenty-three."

"You do?" The guy's eyebrows shot up almost to his hairline. "I'll get the paperwork." The young guy shook his head and while walking off muttered, "There's no accounting for taste anymore."

Ten minutes later Ian held the main door to the pound

open as Alexa and Jana left. "I'll pick Sugar up tomorrow morning."

"Can I come with ya?" Jana slid into the backseat of Ian's white, four-door car.

"Sure." Ian opened the front passenger door for Alexa and mouthed the words *Thank you.*

She gave him a smile before climbing into his vehicle. Alexa's whole face lit when she grinned, as though he was special and the only person who had her attention. The warmth from her expression reached deep into his heart, although a brisk north wind had picked up over the past hour. He struggled to remain removed from Alexa and his attraction to her. Tracy's betrayal was too fresh for him to plunge back into the dating world. Where in the world had the idea of dating come from? Panic nipped at him. She was his employee and over a decade younger than him.

He could barely hold his life together, trying to earn a living while raising Jana and giving her what she needed right now—stability, especially when he didn't feel that way inside. He felt as if he were walking on a thin sheet of ice, cracks spreading out from his footsteps. Any second he was sure he would drop into the cold water.

The next afternoon as the other five children arrived for their math lesson, Jana, carrying her new dog, ran to the door and opened it for each one. "I just got her this morning. Her name is Sugar. Alexa and I decided she has dachshund, bulldog, beagle and maybe some bloodhound in her."

Alexa stood back and greeted the students, having met them all the week before. Randy who was eleven arrived first, his hair redder than Jana's. Haley quickly followed right behind him, entering on his heels. Haley and Jana were both ten, but Jana didn't say much to the other girl. After the first two, Dylan, the oldest at twelve, came with his best friend, Brent. The last to arrive at the house was eleven-year-old Ashley, who Jana gravitated toward and sat next to during the lessons, conducted in the classroom by Ian.

Jana passed Sugar to Ashley. "Isn't she cute?"

Her friend cuddled the small dog. "I love her," while all the other kids said the appropriate words, but their wary looks indicated they thought the animal was a drowned hairless rat that they preferred not to touch.

With Sugar in her arms, Jana started back to the classroom where everyone had headed. Alexa stepped into her path. "I'll take Sugar while you're doing your math lesson."

"Ah, Alexa, she'll help me learn better."

"Just how is she gonna do that?"

Jana rolled her eyes toward the ceiling and contemplated that question for a good twenty seconds. "She calms me when I hold her. You know how anxious I get with math."

"Oh, I see. Do you think your father will approve?"

"Yes—" the child's gaze dropped to the floor "—no. He'll make me put her in her crate and I don't like to see her in jail."

"Jail?" Alexa laughed. "I guess the crate can seem like that, but your dad thought it was a good idea. A lot of people use them."

"Hey, Jana, the class is waiting." Ian approached them in the foyer. "We're going to tackle subtracting fractions today."

"Oh, goodie." The corners of the child's mouth drooped, and she hugged Sugar to her even closer.

Ian peered at Alexa with a frustrated look, as though to say, "See what I'm dealing with concerning math?"

"I'll take Sugar for a walk while you work on math," Alexa said, aware the whole time that Ian stared at her. The warmth from his look sent a zing down her spine.

"Fine." Jana gently plopped Sugar into Alexa's arms and stalked off toward the classroom.

"Thanks. I'm beginning to think this pet idea isn't a good thing. Since she brought Sugar home, the dog has been attached to my daughter. How did you get any work done earlier?"

"We did activities that didn't require the use of both her arms." Alexa chuckled. "I have to admit, it was getting hard to think of things to do. Hey, if you're doing fractions, you might try having them measure different objects. Maybe first have them estimate how long the objects might be, then total them all up. After that, you can have them find the differences between the objects." Right before the kids showed up, she'd seen on the dry eraser board the ten math problems, involving a few addition ones and the rest subtraction. *Dry* was the optimum word here.

"I shouldn't start with the board problems?"

"Hands-on at the beginning can help them learn the concept faster, then use the problems on the board to review."

Ian kneaded the back of his neck. "What objects?"

"Any—books, desks, a windowsill. They don't even have to be in the classroom."

A smile slowly graced Ian's mouth, and he stepped closer. "Thanks. I'll try it. Maybe it will help Jana and Ashley. They have a harder time with math than the others."

"Maybe Ashley could stay after the others leave, and I can help reinforce what you teach both of them."

"That would be perfect. Jana really likes Ashley. I'll talk to her mother today when she comes to pick her up. You're just full of good ideas." He touched her arm briefly, squeezing it, before he spun on his heel and hurried back to the classroom.

Alexa stared at the place where his hand had been on her

as though it had left a mark on her skin. Maybe not a visible one, but definitely in five days since she had come to the house, he'd left one on her heart. Although his outlook on life was different, he was kind and loving toward his daughter. How could a person not respond to that?

Yeah, that's it. I would react to anyone like him. There's nothing really special about Ian. Just a single dad trying to do his best.

Alexa rubbed her cheek against Sugar. "I guess it's you and me for the next hour."

Suddenly the six children flew out of the classroom, all going in different directions. Jana rushed to Alexa, petted her dog, then started for her dad's office.

"What's going on, Jana?"

The young girl swiveled, grinning. "Dad wants us to find something to measure. Anything in the house we can carry back to the classroom. I'm getting his telescope." The child began to turn, stopped in midmotion and swung back toward Alexa. "On second thought, I've got a better idea." She ran to Alexa, snatched Sugar from her grasp and kept going, saying over her shoulder, "She'll be perfect to measure."

"But—" Alexa's words came to a halt. Ian's daughter was already back in the classroom.

Alexa arrived at the door into the room, stepping to the side as the other kids poured back inside with various items to measure. Randy lugged a sofa cushion and plopped it down on his desk, while Haley carried in an oblong planter. When Alexa peeked in, Ian's wide-eyed gaze connected with hers. The look in his eyes shouted the words *What have you gotten me into?*

He crossed to her. "Okay, I probably shouldn't have said, 'let's see how big a number we can get.'"

Alexa laughed. "Are you okay with Jana using Sugar?"

"Yeah, why not? I fear I've lost control of the lesson anyway."

"Do you want me to stay and help?"

"Please. I think I'm in over my head."

For a few seconds his gaze met hers and Alexa *knew* she was in over her head.

Chapter Five

Jana tapped her finger against her chin and made a full circle in the classroom. "I hate this room."

Alexa looked up from the student desk she sat in next to Jana's. "You do?" Maybe now she could do something about the place. After spending over a week in here, she was ready to spend her own money, as scarce as it was, to redecorate the classroom.

"Dad was so proud of fixing up this spare bedroom, I didn't say anything to him."

"I will if you want."

"Great." Jana plopped down in her desk. "I'd love to paint the walls hot pink."

Hot pink! Thinking about the living room done in black and white, Alexa could imagine what Ian would say to that. "Let me see what he has to say."

"What?" Ian stuck his head through the doorway, dressed in his overcoat, his car keys in his hand.

Alexa slowly turned toward him. The sight of him stole her breath every time—which she didn't understand since they were polar opposites. He was nothing like Daniel, her high school sweetheart. And why was she even comparing them? He was her employer. He was much older than she was. They didn't agree on much—well, except about wanting to help Jana. But she had to admit since eight days ago when she'd come to work with the young girl, they were becoming acquainted and fitting into a loose routine, which pleased Ian. Having a schedule had its advantages in keeping Jana on track.

"We were just talking," Jana said to fill the sudden silence.

"Yeah, about maybe doing something to this room to make it more appealing." Alexa rose, gesturing toward the walls. "Maybe paint them a hot pink."

For a few seconds Ian's mouth fell open. "Hot pink." The words exploded from his mouth.

"How about instead of painting, Jana and I go to the store and buy some posters for the walls?"

He pinched the bridge of his nose right above his wire-rimmed glasses as though he had a headache. "Posters? What kind?"

"Something to interest kids. Something Jana likes."

"I don't know—"

"Please, Dad. Alexa and I can go today. Ashley's told me about a neat store downtown called Pop Art and More."

Alexa looked at Jana. "Oh, I love that place. We should find something there."

"I can't go right now. I've got an appointment."

"If you aren't going to be too long, you could drop us off then come back and pick us up." Alexa slid another glance toward Jana to see if she would object.

The young girl blinked, her face going pale, but she didn't say anything.

"I guess I could. I shouldn't be more than half an hour. Okay, Jana?"

Jana nodded slowly, her hands balling at her sides.

Thirty minutes later, Alexa and Jana were flipping through the posters at Pop Art and More and had selected four already. Each one was of a famous place on different continents. When Alexa spied the statue of Christ the Redeemer in Rio de Janeiro, she paused, a warmth suffusing her as she took in the sight of an almost one-hundred-foot-tall Jesus with his arms outstretched as though he was drawing the whole world to him. In the background were the azure blue water and Sugarloaf Mountain at the mouth of Guanabara Bay.

Alexa tapped the poster. "I hope I can see that one day in person."

"Where is it?"

"Brazil."

"Where the Amazon is?"

"Yeah, it's one of the largest countries in the world."

"I don't know anything about Brazil, but I know the Amazon has a lot of unusual animals."

Alexa pulled the rolled-up poster from its bin. "Would you like to learn about the Amazon and Brazil?"

Jana smiled. "Yeah, it would be fun."

"Then we will."

"We will? Don't ya have to ask Dad first?"

"I'll talk to him." Every evening they discussed what Jana was learning, what worked and didn't, where Jana was having a problem, but so far he hadn't objected to what she did with his daughter since that first day.

Jana glanced at her watch. "Dad should be outside by now."

Alexa and Jana headed for the cashier. After Alexa paid for the purchases, using the money Ian had given her, she and Jana left the store. Ian had told them he would park next to the building, and if they weren't outside, he'd come inside. They stood near the entrance of the parking lot and waited for him to show up.

"We can hang these up when we get home." Alexa checked the area for Ian's car.

Jana chewed her fingernail and didn't say anything.

For the next fifteen minutes Alexa tried to keep up a running dialogue about some of the animals she knew lived in the jungles of Brazil, but as the seconds ticked away with no Ian, Jana began pacing, her teeth worrying her bottom lip.

"Where's Dad? He should have been here by now."

"He'll be here. The traffic is heavy."

Jana made another trip to the curb, searched both directions, then came back to Alexa. She curled her hands then uncurled them. "Please call him. Something might be wrong."

Alexa dug into her large purse and retrieved her cell, then punched in Ian's number. Jana stepped closer, concern etched into her features as the phone rang. When he didn't answer and Alexa was switched to voice mail, the color in Jana's face drained. "Ian, Jana and I are outside the store waiting for you. Call back." Alexa flipped it closed and faced Jana, taking her hand.

"I knew it. Something's wrong. I…" The thickness of the child's voice, the tears glistening in her eyes attested to her agitation.

"He's probably still in his meeting and turned his phone off."

Jana shook her head. "No. No."

Alexa wound her arm around the young girl's shoulders. "What animal would you like to investigate first?"

"I—I—"

Alexa's cell rang. She quickly answered it and nodded toward Jana, mouthing the words *your dad*.

"I was on the phone and missed your call. I'm only a block away. Be there in less than a minute."

"Great. See you in a sec."

When Alexa hung up, Jana sagged against Alexa. "I thought something had happened to him."

"It's not gonna happen, Jana. Your dad loves you and will be here for you no matter what, but things do happen to delay people. It's okay."

"But what if something does happen to him? I'll be alone."

"You have a lot of people, me for one, who care about you. I'd never let that happen." Alexa wasn't even sure where that conviction came from, but as she said those words, she meant each one.

An hour later Ian nailed the last poster to the wall in the classroom.

"If I may say so, this room looks much better." Alexa stepped back from the Brazil poster and tilted her head from one side to the other.

"Yeah, *much* better." His daughter stood next to Alexa.

"Okay. Okay, you two. I get it. I shouldn't be in charge of decorating any place."

Jana giggled.

"But hot-pink walls? You two have to admit that's a bit much." Ian faced his daughter and Alexa.

Jana lifted her chin. "Nope. Maybe I can paint my bedroom hot pink."

"Or at least add some posters," Alexa said with a grin and a wink at Ian.

The smile went straight to his heart. In that moment he realized he would really have to work to resist Alexa Michaels. She had been in his house for just over a week and already things were changing. And he didn't like change. The past fifteen months had been one series of changes after another—enough to last a lifetime. So why was it that all the changes Alex brought about made him want to smile?

Jana crossed to the picture of the statue of Christ and ran her hand over it. "Yeah, like this one from Brazil. Alexa, I can see why you'd like to go there one day." Then she turned to the one beside it. "Or this one. I'd love to see Australia."

"Me, too. And Africa. Think of the animals you could see there. One day I'll go. That's my dream."

The enthusiasm in Alexa's voice made Ian scan each poster. Every one of them was of a different country in the world. He hadn't really noticed that as they were putting them up. "You want to travel?"

Alexa's gaze fixed on the poster of Brazil. "More than just to visit, I want to live in other places. There is so much to experience and see. Have you ever been anywhere outside the United States?"

"No."

Jana's forehead creased. "Why not?"

"Because…" He hadn't ever thought about it. "I've been to Hawaii."

"Dad, that doesn't count. It's part of our country."

"I know, but it took eight hours in a plane to get there. I discovered I don't like to fly, especially that long." He'd had to turn control over to a pilot and that hadn't sat well with him.

"I haven't flown, but I would like to." Jana moved from one poster to the next, studying each one.

"Where would you go first?" Alexa asked as she came up behind his daughter, standing in front of a picture of the Alps in Switzerland.

"I don't know."

"By the time we learn about different countries, maybe you can answer that."

Jana whirled. "Yeah. Let's start right now with Brazil."

"Okay. We can start with an online search. Maybe then go to the library and check out some books on Brazil."

"The library." Jana peered at her father, a shadow in her eyes.

"I can go with you two when you're ready if you like, or you can go with Alexa. It'll be your choice."

Jana nodded then headed for the computer set up on a table before the window.

"I'll leave you all to work." He glanced around the class-room. "I actually like the posters."

Alexa's gaze seized his. "I do, too."

The smile that graced her lips tightened his gut. She covered the distance to Jana and sat beside her. He stepped toward the door, paused and peered back at Alexa—then forced himself to look away. Too young for him. What she wanted to do with her life was nothing like his. He'd never thought much about traveling, greeting each day with something different. He liked his familiar everyday existence—where he knew what to expect.

"Dad! Dad, where are you?"

Jana's frantic tone sent a bolt of alarm through Ian. He surged to his feet and hurried into the kitchen. Her pale face and tear-filled eyes alerted him that something was defi-nitely wrong. "What's the matter?"

"Sugar ran off. I was sitting on the bench by the lake, watching the geese and ducks. She was sitting in my lap. A squirrel chasing another one came by, and she leaped off and began racing after them, barking. I tried catching her leash. I couldn't. She ran into the underbrush by the woods." More tears welled in her eyes and a few slid down her cheeks. "I can't lose her."

"We'll go search for her."

"Just us? She may be long gone. She hasn't even been here three weeks yet. She probably doesn't know her way home. Let's call Alexa. She'll come help."

Ian glanced at the kitchen wall clock. "Hon, it's Sunday. Her day off."

"We need people to help. I can go next door and get Kelly. She'll help, too. Plee—ese, Dad, call Alexa." Jana swiped at her wet cheeks.

"Fine."

He strode to the phone and dialed Alexa's cell. Like Jana, he knew she would come if she could. Alexa and his daughter had bonded over the past three weeks. So much, he didn't know how Jana would react when it was time for Alexa to leave at the end of April.

Alexa answered on the second ring. "Yes," she whispered.

He heard people talking in the background. "This is Ian. Is this a bad time?"

"I'm in church at a class. Is something wrong?"

"Sugar ran off. Jana and I are going to look for her. Jana wanted to know if you'd help us."

A long pause and a sound as if she cupped the phone, followed by muffled voices, then she came back on and said, "Yeah, we'll be there. Mom wants to come, too."

"We'll be out back. I'm going to check along the lakeshore. Thanks, Alexa. It means a lot to Jana." *To me.* She wasn't just an employee but a friend, one who made him laugh, made him forget about Tracy's betrayal. That scared him. What did they really have in common except he could tell she cared about his daughter?

That actually meant a lot to him. Was it enough?

* * *

Alexa arrived at Ian and Jana's house fifteen minutes later with her mother. After parking in the driveway, she threw open her door and hurriedly stood. "They'll be around back. I hope they've found Sugar." She started for the side yard.

"Yeah, me, too. I don't know how much hiking I can do in heels." Gloria jogged to keep up with Alexa. "Slow down a tad. Three-inch heels aren't meant for running."

Alexa peered over her shoulder. "Sorry. I'm worried about Jana and what she'll do if we can't find Sugar. She's become so attached to that dog."

"I don't know why. It's ugly." Her mother slowed, dragging in deep breaths.

"That's what I think makes Sugar so adorable."

"I think I should have taken you to the eye doctor when you were younger. Maybe you should see one, dear. The dog doesn't any hair to speak of."

In the back near the lake, Alexa stopped, cupped her hand above her eyes to see past the glare off the glittering water and scanned the area. "Do you see either Jana or Ian?"

Her mom pointed to the left. "I see them. They're coming back."

Alexa twisted around. Empty-handed, the pair hiked toward them. The fear on Jana's face tore at Alexa. Even Ian's held concern, especially when he glanced at his daughter. His unconditional love for his daughter moved Alexa. She didn't have that with her own father. Seeing it between Jana and Ian caused her to wonder what it would be like to be loved with no strings attached. Ian made her dream of that kind of love.

"Nothing that way." Ian paused next to Alexa. "That's the direction Sugar went."

"Kelly and her younger brother went that way." Jana

pointed to the right. "We need more people to check the woods."

"We came back to get you to help us look." Ian settled his arm along Jana's shoulders and pulled her against him.

"What if we don't find Sugar before dark? She'll get scared. Be hungry." The child's eyes, red rimmed, glistened with her unshed tears.

"We will, honey, if I have to stay out here all day." Ian kissed the top of Jana's head.

Alexa watched the interchange between Ian and his daughter, her own tears cramming her throat. Never once in her childhood had her father ever acted that way toward her. He'd rarely hugged her or showed her that kind of affection. Ian's capability to love was huge and he had no problem showing it.

Alexa swallowed several times. "And I'll be right there next to you all, searching for Sugar. We're gonna find her." She rotated toward her mother. "Why don't you stay here, and when Kelly and her brother come back, tell them where we are."

"I can help with the search in the woods."

Alexa pointed to her mother's shoes. "In those?" How she could wear three-inch high heels at all was beyond her. She was glad she'd changed her mind at the last minute and worn boots, instead of flats, to church today. "Besides, Sugar may find her way home, or someone might call to say they've found her. Someone needs to be here. If anything happens, call me on my cell."

"There's Kelly and her brother." Jana ran toward the two coming along the shoreline from the opposite direction.

"And no Sugar," Ian said with a sigh, staring at his daughter greeting the two neighbors. "I've got to find that dog."

Alexa moved in front of him. "*We've* got to find the dog."

He blinked, focused on her and attempted a smile that failed instantly. "Thanks. I've learned I can count on you."

"Jana's a delight, and I don't want to see her hurting. If we don't find Sugar in the woods, then we'll extend our search. Some of the other neighbors might help, too." Alexa took his hands. "Sugar isn't a dog that blends in. She's unusual. That will help us in our search."

One corner of his mouth tugged upward. "So I should be glad she is so ugly."

"Yeah, something like that."

"Dad, Kelly and Aaron are gonna help us search the woods. Let's go." Jana trudged toward the grove of trees, flanked by the two teens.

"Thanks, Gloria, for staying here. The back door is open if you get cold." Ian released one of Alexa's hands but kept hold of the other one and started after the kids.

"Did you ever have a pet as a child?" Alexa asked, to take her mind off the fact that the warmth of his grasp had sent her heart pounding.

"No, my mother didn't want to have any pets in the house. Too messy for her."

"Are your parents alive?"

"My dad died a few years back from cancer. My mother lives in Florida with her sister. How about your father? You never talk about him."

"My father is alive but doesn't want to have much to do with me." The words were out before she could stop them. In all the time she had lived in Tallgrass, she hadn't told anyone about her father's rejection, the conditions he put on his love. The hurt burrowed deep in her heart came to the foreground.

"Why? What happened?" He slowed his pace.

Ian's question, spoken with such concern, gave her yet

another reason she was drawn to him. He cared and wasn't afraid to show it. "I didn't want to become a doctor like him. My dad wasn't happy with my choice of occupation. I haven't seen him in five years."

"I'm sorry. That can't be easy for you." He paused, his intense gaze on her.

The look in his eyes pulled her closer, as though she didn't have a will of her own. For a long moment she forgot they were following Jana. All Alexa's senses became centered on Ian. His touch on her. His musky scent that competed with the outdoor aromas of the trees and lake. Her heartbeat slammed against her rib cage in a mad staccato. He edged closer, lifting his hand toward her face as he leaned forward. He palmed her cheek, his mouth inches away.

Jana calling out to them separated Alexa and Ian.

"I…" Words evaded her.

A flushed stained his cheeks. He spun on his heel and resumed his trek toward the woods.

Alexa quickened her step and caught up with him. "Jana is lucky to have you."

"But she still has to deal with a parent's rejection, and nothing I can do will change that fact." A frown descended, his jaw clenched.

She snagged his hand and squeezed it, trying to convey her silent support as they approached the kids standing at the edge of the woods.

"We've been talking. We need to split up and cover as much of the area as possible," Kelly said as she surveyed the grove of pine and scrub oak.

"Yeah. Kelly, Aaron and me are going that way." Jana waved her arm toward the left. "You two go to the right. We'll meet on the other side."

"If we find Sugar, I've got my cell. I'll call you, Mr.

Ferguson." Kelly started forward with Aaron and Jana quickly catching up.

Alexa stared after their disappearing figures for a moment, then looked at Ian.

"I think my daughter has actually learned something from me. I didn't realize she could take charge like that. Usually she's disorganized and apathetic, especially this past year."

"She wants to find Sugar badly. She's smart and can do anything she sets her mind to. I found the unit on animals we're doing has sparked a lot of interest in Jana. I want to suggest we go to the ranch Helping Hands Homeschooling Group uses. Will that be okay?"

"If you can get my daughter to agree, that would be great."

The weary lines on his face tugged at Alexa. "You might have to go with us at least the first time."

"Fine by me. I've been trying, and she hasn't wanted to."

"When was the last time you asked her?" Alexa strode toward the right, several yards separating her and Ian as they moved through the stand of trees.

Cocking his head, he thought a moment. "Last November. I guess with Christmas and my business picking up, it slipped my mind."

"I'm gonna tie it in with our animal unit and try to persuade her."

Ian cupped his hand around his mouth and shouted, "Sugar. Sugar."

Alexa followed suit, yelling the pet's name every few yards and walking farther away from Ian to cover more ground. Fifteen minutes later she emerged on the other side of the woods at the same time that Ian did. He came to her, a grim expression on his face.

"This isn't good," he said while looking toward the

area where the kids would appear after they completed their search.

"Maybe Jana found Sugar and they forgot to call."

"Maybe." But his tight voice showed his doubts. "I'm going to have to prepare myself for the possibility Sugar is lost for good."

"If that's the case, there were a lot of dogs at the pound. I'm sure there's another—"

"No! I'm not setting my daughter up for another letdown. Once is enough."

The vehemence between his declarations made Alexa wonder if he was expressing his feelings, especially since his wife had walked out on them. He'd suffered great disappointment and hurt because of another he'd loved. She could understand that he didn't want to risk that pain again. Although Daniel hadn't left her, he'd died and the end result had been that she had been left alone.

Alexa started to say something, when Jana, Kelly and Aaron came into view. Each of them wore a frown. When Jana ran to her dad and flung her arms around him, she began to cry.

"We'll keep looking, pumpkin."

"We need more people to help." Alexa patted the young girl on the back. "And I've got just the people. I belong to a singles group at church. We have a calling tree. I'll make a call and see who I can get here to assist in scouring the area. Sugar is small. Maybe she's scared, and since she hasn't been Sugar for long, she could have forgotten her new name."

Jana pulled back and looked up at Alexa. "Yeah. She was learning it, but she didn't always come to it."

While Alexa took out her cell to make the call to Dr. Nancy Baker, also a member of the singles group at church, Kelly stepped forward. "Me and Aaron will go door to door and tell the neighbors what's going on. If they can help search, great. If not, at least we can describe Sugar and let them know to be on the lookout for her. Want to come with us, Jana?"

Jana bit her teeth into her lower lip. "I don't know."

"That's okay. Aaron and me can do it." Kelly began walking toward the street a few hundred feet away.

Jana peered up at her dad, her brow furrowed.

"You can stay with me if you want, hon, but I'll be helping Alexa organize her group when they arrive."

"Wait, Kelly. I'm coming with you." Jana loped to her friends and joined them.

When Nancy came on the phone, Alexa explained what was going on, then hung up. "She'll start the calling tree, and then she'll come over to help so we have at least one extra volunteer."

He took her hand. "Let's get back to the house. I have a few pictures of Sugar on my digital camera. I'll need to run some off for the searchers."

"Great. Although Sugar is distinctive, a photo would be better than a description."

As they made their way back to Ian's, their hands remained clasped, even when one of her mother's eyebrows rose as she watched them traverse the backyard. Alexa knew her mom would have a lot of questions about Ian and her later, when things settled down. The problem was it was becoming more difficult to say it was only an employer/employee relationship. He'd almost kissed her. And the fact he hadn't had disappointed her.

Exhausted, Alexa twisted away from the window at Ian's house, having stared out into the darkness so long she began to imagine Sugar racing across the backyard toward the patio. The last group of searchers had reported in half an hour ago. No Sugar. Crying, Jana had run to her bedroom and slammed the door. Ian had gone after her to talk to her. Even several rooms away, occasionally she heard Jana's sobs, and her own sadness enveloped her. She wouldn't leave until she knew Jana was calmer.

A sound behind Alexa drew her toward it. Ian stood in the entrance to the den. His weariness carved bleak lines into his face. The pain in his eyes ripped all her defenses to shreds. Not just Jana needed her. Ian did, too. He'd been equally the reason she'd decided to stay after everyone else had left.

"What am I going to do?"

"Be there for Jana. That's all you can do." And he was very good at that.

"I can't talk to her. All she does is cry. She didn't cry this much when her mother left last year. I tried to tell her we could look some more tomorrow—call animal shelters and the pound, put up posters." He moved into the middle of the room. "I feel helpless. She wanted me to leave."

"She's hurting. Give her a few minutes, and then maybe she'll listen to what you're saying."

"Maybe. She wanted a new dog if Sugar doesn't come home. I don't know if I can go through this again. I don't know if I should set her up for more pain."

She covered the distance between them and took his hands. "I know it's tough to care about something, someone. It can be taken away suddenly."

His solemn eyes connected with hers. "You're young and have just begun to—"

"I had a guy, Daniel, I loved deeply in high school." Sadness momentarily swelled in her, and she stepped away. "It was only a month away from our graduation. We'd planned to marry the next year, and he died in a freak accident." She snapped her fingers. "Just like that, gone. So I know. Age has nothing to do with suffering. My—experience has made me look at things differently."

A tic jerked in his hard jawline. "I don't know what else to say to her. I wish we'd never gotten the dog."

"Dad! How can you say that?" Jana screamed from the doorway, then whirled around and fled.

Ian stood frozen, watching his daughter disappear. "I didn't mean…"

"Let me go talk to her. Maybe I can help."

A door slammed closed, and Ian winced. "Please. I've certainly messed this all up."

In her trek toward Jana's bedroom, Alexa paused beside Ian and touched his arm. "Parents can't always shield their children from being hurt." She continued across the den, then into the kitchen and finally the hallway.

At Jana's door, she knocked.

"Go away. I don't want to talk to you, Dad."

"Jana, it's me. Can I come in?"

A long minute ticked by one excruciatingly slow second at a time. Finally the door swung open. A teary-eyed Jana backed away. "Come in."

"How much of the conversation did you hear?"

"Enough to know that Dad didn't want Sugar. I know she messed things up. Chewed some of his papers, but I love her."

Alexa crossed to the bed and eased down. After being on her feet most of the day, she didn't know if she could stand much longer. "You can ask him, but what I think he meant when he said that was he didn't want to see you hurt again if something happened to another dog."

Jana plopped down next to Alexa, tears making her eyes shiny. "You think Sugar is gone for good?"

"Actually no, I don't. I think we'll find her."

"You're just saying that."

"Why don't we pray together for her return. That'll help our chances of getting her back."

"Pray—like to God?"

"He's the only one. He's the one we should turn to in our time of need, and I think this is a need."

"How do we do that?"

Alexa took Jana's hand. "I'll show you. Speak from your heart. Tell Him what you want. Let Him know how much Sugar means to you." She bowed her head.

"Can you start it for me?" Jana followed Alexa's action, dropping her chin almost to her chest.

"Heavenly Father, Jana has a request that means a lot to her. Please help her."

After a half a minute's pause, Jana murmured, "Please, please bring Sugar home to me. I love her and don't want anything to happen to her. She's probably scared right now. If You help me, I'll go to church every week. I'll do whatever You want. Amen." Jana lifted her head. "Let's go see if she's back yet."

"Honey, it doesn't always happen like that. He works in His time, not ours. Be patient."

"But if I pray for something, God will give it to me?"

"God is like all parents. His answer sometimes is yes and sometimes no. Or, He'll want you to wait if the time isn't right at that moment. He knows what's best even though we don't always. But He wants to hear from you, your dreams, your problems, your desires. That's what praying is. It never hurts to do it." Rising, Alexa offered the child her hand. "Tell you what. Let's do what we can to help get Sugar back as fast as possible. We can make posters and then tomorrow we can put them up around town. That's if you want."

"Yes." Jana leaped off the bed.

"You don't have to bargain with God by promising to do something like go to church for your prayer to be answered, but if you want to go to church, I go every Sunday. I'd love to have you go with me."

"You don't think Dad would go?"

"You'll have to ask him."

"Probably not. He stopped when Mom left."

Alexa started for the hallway. "There's only one way to find out."

"I think he's mad at God. Do you think that will make a difference to God?"

"No. He's willing to forgive anyone who asks." *And He wants us to forgive, too, and yet I can't.* The rejection of her father had buried itself even deeper into her heart, especially when she'd seen the hurt her mother was going through.

"Let's go make those posters." Alexa settled her hand on Jana's shoulder as they made their way to the family room.

Ian turned when they walked into the den. Hope flared in his eyes as he looked at his daughter. "Are you all right?"

"Yes, Alexa and I are gonna make posters about Sugar, then put them up tomorrow. She'll be coming home. I know it—" Jana tapped her chest "—in here."

Concern marked Ian's expression.

"Jana, why don't you go get some paper from the classroom. I had some on the desk I think will work for the posters. And bring some markers." As soon as the child left, Alexa faced Ian, preparing herself for his question.

"What did you say to her?"

"I gave her hope. We prayed to the Lord and asked Him to bring Sugar home."

"He's not going to answer that prayer."

"Why not?"

"Because He's obviously too busy to deal with small— or for that matter, large—family matters."

Alexa lifted her chin. "You don't know that. I also gave her something to do to help bring Sugar home. We're gonna make posters. I hope you'll help us."

He glared at her, but kept his mouth shut because Jana came back into the den with the supplies. The young girl sat at the round game table by the bay window and spread the paper and pens out.

"Dad, you want to help us?"

"Sure, pumpkin. In fact, let me run off some more pictures of Sugar, and we can put a photo on each poster."

"Great idea!" Jana picked up a black marker. "What should we put on this, Alexa?"

While his daughter and Alexa sat side by side, Ian slipped out of the den and hurried to his office where he began running off copies of the photo he'd used earlier. He sank into his chair behind his desk while the printer churned out forty pictures.

Anger surged through him. How could Alexa do that? Raise his daughter's hopes only to have it dashed tomorrow or the next day when Jana realized the Lord wasn't going to bring her pet home? He'd have to pick up the pieces of Jana's broken heart, not Alexa, not God. Just like he had when Tracy had left them.

He'd asked the Lord to bring his wife home, to help him make everything all right. But she hadn't returned. His life had totally changed. And he'd had to deal with Jana's pain, with his own pain.

How was he going to make this better for his daughter? How was he going to fix this latest disaster? No matter how much he tried to control what was happening, it seemed to fall apart without a moment's notice.

His elbows on his desk, Ian removed his glasses and massaged the area between his eyes, then scrubbed his hands down his face as the sound of the printer reminded him why he was in his office.

"Ian?"

He slowly raised his head and gave Alexa a piercing look.

"I'm sorry." Alexa moved into the office and stood before his desk. "I didn't mean to make you mad or overstep my boundaries."

He gripped the arms of his chair. "Ever since you've come into my house, you've overstepped your boundaries. Why should this be any different?"

His words hurt. She tried to squelch that feeling, knowing he was lashing out because he was worried about his daughter, but she couldn't. She gritted her teeth, afraid if she spoke she would say something that would make the situation even worse.

"What happens if Sugar never comes home?"

"She'll be found."

"You don't know that."

"Yes, I do. I just feel it."

Ian bolted to his feet. "I'm the one who'll have to deal with my daughter's tears and hurt, her disappointment in the Lord when He doesn't bring Sugar home."

His furious words blasted her in the face although they were spoken in almost a whisper. "Why are you so sure He won't?"

Chapter Six

Balling his hands on his desk, Ian leaned across it. "Because He's let me down. He doesn't care about what we're going through. I'm certainly not worth His attention."

"That's not true. He cares. He loves every one of His children."

"I haven't seen any evidence of it lately. Praying didn't help me. Now Jana will think all she has to do is pray and she'll get what she wants."

"I've explained what I think praying is, and it's certainly not getting your every heart's desire."

Ian snatched up the stack of copies from the printer and headed for the door. "Let's go make these posters." His rigid posture, his long strides, attested to the anger that still seized Ian as he left his office.

Alexa sighed. All she'd wanted to do was help Jana. Maybe she wasn't the right person for this job. Doubts attacked her from all sides as she made her way toward the family room.

"Look, Alexa, I've almost finished the first poster." Jana took the top picture of Sugar from the pile Ian laid on the table. "All I have to do is glue this to the paper and it will be ready."

Alexa sat next to Jana. "I like what you've done."

"Dad, how many do you think we should make?" Jana peered at him then swung her gaze to Alexa then back to her father. "Is everything all right?"

One corner of his mouth hitched up. His dimple appeared, although from the reserved look in his eyes, the grin was forced. "It will be, when Sugar comes home." He picked up a blank piece of paper. "I think we should make thirty or thirty-five, then if we need more we can make more."

"That sounds like a plan." Alexa withdrew a brown marker from the box.

"Yeah." Jana began working on another poster, her head bent over it, her attention totally focused as she printed out the words.

Across the table Ian caught Alex's gaze. The half grin vanished, to be replaced with a cold expression that, as she held his look, melted into a neutral one.

An hour later thirty-five posters were completed and ready to go. Alexa shoved to her feet, arching her back and stretching, she rolled her head in a full circle to ease the tension that had stiffened her whole upper body.

She pushed in her chair. "It's time that I go home, but I'll be back early tomorrow. If it's all right with your dad, after breakfast we can start putting up these posters."

"Fine." Ian rose. "I'll walk you to your car."

"Be here early. We'll be ready to go." Jana stacked the posters in a large pile.

Alexa gathered her purse and jacket from the couch and started for the foyer. Ian's presence behind her caused her tension to return full force and knot her shoulders and neck even more. After opening the front door, she spun around and said, "You don't have to walk me to my car. It's just parked in the driveway."

"I know."

She stepped out onto the porch, and he followed. Hurrying her pace, she crossed the yard while digging around in her oversize purse for her keys. She was emotionally drained and didn't want to engage in any more verbal battle.

As she unlocked her car door and thrust it open, she said, "Thanks. See you tomorrow."

"Alexa, I'm sorry for earlier."

Her jaw dropped, and she straightened to face him. She couldn't think of anything to say to him.

"Your heart is always in the right place where Jana is concerned. I've seen that on more than one occasion. You thought you were doing what was best for my daughter, and I can't fault you for that." He took off his wire-rimmed glasses and rubbed the bridge of his nose. "I'm just worried about Jana and I said things I shouldn't have in my office."

But you meant them. If she was smart, she'd back away from this family, put in her time and leave with her heart intact. "I understand. See you tomorrow, early."

She quickly slid behind the steering wheel, her hands shaking. She wasn't going to be smart. She could tell. She cared about Jana—and Ian—too much. The thought of the almost kiss earlier that day stayed with her as she drove to her house.

By the time she reached home, she'd dismissed what might have happened near the woods and pulled her calm mantle about her, knowing that otherwise her mother would discern something was wrong besides Sugar being lost. Her mom knew how to read her, and Alexa had never been good at hiding her feelings for long. And worse,

Gloria had witnessed the almost kiss. Her mother would want to know how she felt about Ian.

When she entered her duplex, Alexa found her mother waiting for her in the living room. As Charlie got up to greet Alexa, Gloria put the book she was reading on the table next to her.

"You haven't found Sugar yet, have you?" she asked. "I can tell by the look on your face. How's Jana taking it?"

"Okay. We made posters to put up tomorrow around town. I know the neighbors are aware Sugar is missing, but the dog might wander farther away from her home than a six-block radius."

Her mom's assessing gaze skimmed over her features. "And you? How are you?"

"Tired. I'd go straight to bed except I'm still too wired to sleep." *Oops.* The second she had said the last sentence she'd realized her mistake. Her mother would take that as a cue to chat with her about Ian.

"Let me fix you a cup of chamomile tea. It'll relax you and help you sleep."

Alexa trailed her mother into the kitchen and sat at the table while Gloria busied herself putting the water on to boil and getting the tea bags. "Thanks for searching earlier."

"Anything to help." After putting the bags and water into the mugs, she carried them to the table and sat across from Alexa. "I didn't tell you, but your dad called me again on my cell while I was out looking for Sugar. He wanted to talk. I didn't want to have that conversation at Ian's, so I came back here and called him."

"Are you going home?" Alexa cupped her mug between her palms, its warmth seeping into her cold hands.

"This is my home right now. He didn't say anything to

change that." Her mother took a sip of her tea. "I'm thinking I need this more than you," she said, gesturing to the mug. "Every time I talk about that man, I get riled, so let's discuss something else. Are you falling for Ian?"

Alexa spewed her drink of tea. "Mom! Why would you ask that?"

"I saw you two today. I've seen the looks you have exchanged, and I'm worried about you. Don't get involved with him, honey. He's got too much baggage for you." Her mother averted her look, chewing on her lower lip. "Your father had a lot of baggage when we got married."

"He did?"

"I never told you that your dad was married before me. He even had a child before you. A son."

Alexa collapsed back in the chair. The tea sloshed out onto her hand and burned it. She quickly placed the mug on the table and massaged the red spot. "Mom, how about warning me before you drop a bombshell?"

"Sorry."

"Why wasn't I told?"

"Because when he married me, he made me promise never to bring it up. I'm breaking my promise because I'm worried you're following in my footsteps. Look where it has landed me—estranged from my husband."

"My situation with Ian isn't anything like that. Marriage? Where is that coming from?" Although for a few seconds, she began to picture being married to Ian, but pushed those thoughts away as ridiculous. Tonight only confirmed that. They were in different places in their lives, and the faith that meant so much to her was clearly something he couldn't share.

"Ian reminds me of your father in some ways. He's struggling to control his emotions, his life. He's hurting. I didn't see that until after I married your father that he wasn't really over his deceased wife."

"What happened to her?"

"A car accident. A drunk driver took both his wife and baby son. His first wife was a friend from church. I tried to help Richard and, as you know, eventually married him. He wasn't the same man I knew before the accident."

Alexa stood. She had to escape to the privacy of her room. Her thoughts reeled with the news her mother had told her. Her father had a son who'd died. Was that why he didn't love her? Was that why it had been so important that she followed in her father's footsteps?

"You don't need to worry about me, Mom. I'm not falling in love with Ian. I'm aware he has issues with his ex-wife, and he's certainly not ready to be involved in a relationship. Tomorrow will be a long day. I'd better go to bed." She turned to leave.

"Hon, you didn't drink your tea."

Alexa glanced back. "I don't need it now." *Because I won't sleep no matter what I drink.*

"Where's Jana?" Alexa asked when Ian opened the door to her the next morning half an hour before she usually came.

"Out back. She's been on the bench since I woke up this morning, waiting for Sugar to return."

"And she hasn't?"

"No. When I went out to tell her breakfast was ready, she told me she wasn't hungry."

"Is it okay if I go and talk to her?"

"Sure. She told me to let her know when you came."

She started for the door that opened onto the patio.

"Alexa, do you want some tea? I have hot water for it."

His question stopped her halfway across the den. About

a week ago he'd started putting a kettle of water on the stove for her to use throughout the day. He'd even stocked her favorite teas. The gesture had warmed her the week before; now she didn't have the energy to care one way or another. With practically no sleep, all she could manage was going through the motions of her day and hope she could rid her mind of the conversations she'd had with Ian and her mother the night before.

She headed back to the kitchen. "Yes, thanks." Although she'd had some tea at home, she needed as much caffeine as she could get. After grabbing a mug with her drink already steeping, she left the house.

Across the backyard sat Jana on the bench Ian had made. She stared at the water, huddled in a blanket around her slumped shoulders as though she'd gotten up from bed and come straight outside with her covers. Alexa's heart grew heavy at the sight of the child, so forlorn looking.

"Good morning, Jana."

"She hasn't come back yet."

Alexa settled on the bench next to the child. "Then after breakfast we'll do what we can. We'll call the pound and animal shelters to put them on alert if they find her. We'll put up all those posters. Let people know we're looking for her."

"But we did that yesterday and no one's called."

"By the time we get through we'll have the whole town aware Sugar's missing. We just need to get the word out even more."

"Yeah." Jana brightened, sitting up a little straighter. "The more people looking, the better the chance she'll be found."

"She hasn't even been gone twenty-four hours."

"It seems longer."

"Let's go eat breakfast and then we can get started."

Jana hopped up, hiking the blanket up enough so it didn't drag across the grass, and hurried toward the patio.

By the time Alexa entered the house, Jana was sitting at the kitchen table, gulping down her orange juice, then pouring milk over her cereal. Alexa took the seat across from Jana and finally sipped her tea.

"Do you want anything to eat?" Ian asked as he brought his coffee and toast to the table.

"No, I'm fine."

"Slow down, Jana," Ian said as she shoveled the cereal into her mouth. "We aren't leaving until I'm finished with my breakfast. Then I have to make two calls to postpone a couple of meetings. After that, I'm all yours."

"Alexa and me can go without ya. We can meet ya in town later."

Ian's eyes widened. "Fine," he said slowly.

A few minutes later, Jana scraped back her chair and stood. "I'm ready. I'll get the posters. They're in my room." She raced toward the hallway.

"A girl on a mission." Ian shook his head. "I can't believe she's leaving with you and not waiting for me."

"She's focused on bringing Sugar back home. She's forgotten her fear for the moment."

"I'm sorry Sugar is gone and believe me I want her to be returned home, but I'll take this breakthrough any way I can get it. You'll be the first person she's gone with since summer without me tagging along."

As Alexa rose from the table, so did Ian. He captured her hand. "Thanks for being here. A month ago I would have said this situation wouldn't have worked."

"You did say that. You didn't hire me at first."

"Yeah, well…" The sound of Jana returning drew his gaze toward the entrance. He released her hand. "How about I meet you two in front of the courthouse at the square? I should be there in thirty minutes. I'll have to give one client a chance to make it to his office. Will you be all right even if I'm a little late?"

Jana pressed her lips together for a moment, her brows knitted. "Yeah, but call if you're gonna be too late. Ready, Alexa?"

"We'll need tape, a hammer and nails."

"I know where some are." Jana handed Alexa the posters and hurried toward the garage.

Ian watched his daughter disappear from view. "What if this doesn't work?"

"My motto is that I won't worry about something until it's a problem. Wasted energy."

"I like to plan for every contingency."

"Why?"

"No surprises."

"I love surprises. Keeps life exciting." Except the one she'd discovered last night from her mother. Her parents should have told her, or at least her father, that he'd had a previous wife and son.

"I've had my fair share of surprises, and I don't relish them."

"Surprises can be good. Besides, think of all that stress you can avoid because only one of those contingencies will come true. Wait and see which one. You'll live longer."

He chuckled. "I don't see myself changing. I'll exercise instead."

Alexa warmed beneath Ian's gaze. She swallowed hard, the restless night before coming to mind. He was part of the reason.

Jana returned from the garage. "I've got everything. Let's go."

As Alexa crossed the kitchen, she peered back at Ian and smiled. "See you in a little bit."

The assessing look he sent her raised goose bumps as she left and accompanied her thoughts all the way to her car. Before she backed out of the driveway, she rubbed her hands up and down her jacket-clad arms, trying to erase his effect on her.

"You know we never talked about the next animal you want to study," Alexa said to Jana to try to take her mind off Ian and the look and smile that had flooded his face as she strolled out of the kitchen.

"I don't know. There are so many I like."

"How about horses?"

"Yeah, I've always wanted to learn to ride ever since I was a little girl."

"When I was growing up, I used to save all my money from birthdays, Christmases and what I earned. I was gonna buy a pony and keep it in the backyard."

"Did ya?"

"No, my dad informed me when I was nine and had saved three hundred dollars that I couldn't get one, even if I kept it somewhere else."

"Why didn't he tell ya before?"

"Because he wanted me to learn the value of saving." Alexa turned onto Main Street.

"Did ya?"

"Yeah, I guess I did." Thinking about that time always aroused her ire, but this time she saw it just a little differently since getting to know Ian and understanding what it was like to be a father. *But he should have told me.*

"Did ya ever learn to ride?"

"No. Your dad told me there's a ranch a lot of the kids in the Helping Hands Homeschooling Group use. Why don't we check into it and see about riding lessons for both of us. It's about time I learned, don't you think?"

Jana chewed on her lower lip. "I don't know. Let me think about it."

Alexa pulled into a parking space near the town square. "I understand the ranch has other animals, too. It would be like a large classroom for us. Think of all the possibilities."

Jana glanced around as though she finally realized she was sitting in a car in the middle of downtown without her father. "Do ya think Dad would come?"

"We'll ask him when he arrives to help us."

"How did last night go?" Alexa asked the next morning when Ian let her into his house.

"Not well. Every time the phone rang she was sure it was someone who'd found Sugar and had seen our number on a poster." Ian sighed. "I'm running out of things to say to her to comfort her. I was so afraid of this."

"It hasn't been that long."

"To a child who's missing her pet, it's been too long. To the parent trying to give her hope, it's been longer than that."

"I think the best thing we can do is try to take her mind off it. Today's a new day. I called the ranch and checked on when we could come out there to see the place. Zachary Rutgers, the owner of the Wild Bill Buffalo Ranch, said any afternoon this week would be fine with him. Do you have an afternoon you could get away for a few hours?"

Ian stepped to the side while she entered the house, then, after shutting the door, turned toward her in the foyer. Raking his fingers through his hair—and from its disheveled look not for the first time that day—he grimaced. "I can Thursday if I move a meeting. That'll be the best day for me."

"Then I'll let Zachary know, if Jana agrees to go."

"Now that I think about it, if I move things around, we can go this afternoon right after lunch. I'll just stay up late tonight and finish what I need to."

That was as close to being spontaneous as Ian had been in the time she'd worked for him. She grinned. "You better watch out. Before you know it, you might not use your day planner."

He laughed. "That will never happen. That day planner keeps me sane. You should try it. It frees me up not to have to keep everything up here." He tapped his temple.

"Is Jana in the kitchen?"

"Nope. The den, staring out the window. At least she's not sitting on the bench outside. That broke my heart yesterday watching her watch for Sugar."

"Well, let me see what she says about the ranch. You might not have to rearrange anything."

"I'll fix you some tea while you talk to her."

"Chicken."

"Yep. You seem to get her to do things I can't, so I bow to your superior persuasive skills." With a twinkling gleam in his eyes, he bent at the waist and swept his arm across his body.

This playful Ian was intriguing. Alexa had to shore up her defenses to keep her feelings from evolving into something that wasn't possible. She wasn't without her own plans. She wanted to travel, work in a third-world country as a teacher. Her gift for languages would assist her in her dream to help others less fortunate. That was what she and Daniel had planned back in high school. She would fulfill his dream as well as her own. She owed it to him for the years they had been together and envisioned their life as a married couple.

In the den Alexa pulled up a seat close to Jana, who sat

in front of the bay window with her elbow on the arm of her chair and her chin in her palm. The urge to wrap her arms around the child swamped her.

"Hey, kiddo. How's it going?" Alexa placed her hand on the girl's shoulder.

"I'm worried. How's Sugar gonna get food to eat?"

"When she gets hungry enough, she'll find her way home." Alexa massaged the tension in the child's shoulders. "In the meantime she wouldn't want you to mope around waiting for her. We're gonna get our schoolwork done this morning because right after lunch you, your dad and I are gonna go to the ranch I told you about. Zachary said he'd give you your first riding lesson this afternoon if you're interested."

"Zachary?"

"He owns the Wild Bill Buffalo Ranch. Did you know he keeps real buffalo on his place?"

"Buffalo? Really?" Jana perked up and straightened in the chair.

"Yep, he has a small herd of them, and we can go see them. Are ya game?"

"Dad's coming?"

"He's clearing his calendar just so he can. Before we go, you can look up quarter horses and buffalo. I know that Zachary has other animals, too. After we return from the ranch, we can list them and do research on them the rest of the week. So are you ready to get to work?"

"Yes!" Jana jumped up from the chair. "I'll get the laptop and we can start right away."

Alexa rose and found Ian in the doorway from the kitchen with two mugs in his hand. He strode across the family room and gave her the one filled with tea. Their hands touched and a tingling zapped up her arm. She nearly dropped her drink and quickly clasped it between both palms.

With a lopsided grin, he said, "I'd better go clear that calendar."

Alexa watched him walk away, his moves economical, not a wasted motion. Like the man. He planned and made everything he did efficient, whereas she often spun her wheels, so to speak, arriving late to some events and early to others. Ian used a day planner and referred to it often. Maybe a day planner wasn't such a bad idea.

The very thought for a few seconds chilled her, as though her father had invaded her life again, demanding she do everything on a schedule. Another remnant of her conversation with her mother Sunday evening—when they had talked about her father.

Chapter Seven

"I guess it didn't hurt that Ashley lives at the ranch." Ian leaned against the railing of the paddock.

"Yeah, I did happen to mention that to Jana as we were putting up posters yesterday." Alexa threw him a glance before returning her attention to his daughter riding her first horse while Zachary gave her some pointers. "I found out from Ashley that she and her family live in one house while Zachary lives in another on the property. Her mother is Zachary's older sister."

"You are quite sneaky and devious."

"I have my moments. It pays to get to know the children." Jana's giggles mingling with Ashley's floated to Alexa. "Now, *that's* a wonderful sound. If anyone can get your daughter to laugh it will be her friend."

"Oh, I don't know. I've heard more laughter in my house over the past month than in a long time. I think you've helped there."

Alexa swerved her full attention to Ian and got caught in the snare of his gaze. His compliment crammed her throat with emotions. He was a man who told people when he felt they were doing a good job. He often let his daughter know how well she was doing. For a moment the ranch faded from her consciousness, and all she could see was him, his face relaxed in a smile, his eyes fastened on her as though Alexa was special—important to him. "Don't you know laughter is the best medicine?"

His grin hitched up another notch. "I heard that somewhere but didn't realize until I met you how true it was."

Why hadn't her father ever told her she was doing a good job? That he loved her? It would have made all the difference in the world. That was why she knew Jana would be all right in time. Ian would make sure of that.

"Dad, look at me," Jana shouted across the paddock. She rode her horse around the ring, and stopped near Ashley sitting on her mount. Then Jana had her mare turn in a full circle. "She does what I say."

"Now, if only I could get my daughter to do that," he whispered to Alexa right before he said to Jana, "You're doing great, and you've only had one lesson. Wait until you have more."

"Ashley wants me to ride with her out in the pasture. Can I?"

"I don't..." Ian blinked then looked at Zachary in the middle of the corral for some help answering his daughter.

"It'll be okay. I'll ride with them. In fact, you two can come along." Zachary, dressed in jeans, a flannel shirt and boots, tipped back his cowboy hat.

"Great." Ian pushed off the railing. "I haven't ridden in years."

Alexa gulped. "I haven't ridden at all. I'd probably better stay put."

"Where's the adventurous side I'm getting to know so well?"

"I think I left that at home today."

He grabbed her hand and tugged her gently closer to the barn's entrance. "Oh, no. Not allowed. If I'm going to get sore then so are you."

"Ian Ferguson, I can't believe you said that." Although her voice sounded stern, she couldn't keep the smile off her face.

The two young girls remained in the corral while Zachary brought two large horses out of the barn. "I have some more kids coming this afternoon, so we'll only be able to ride for half an hour, but that should be enough to hook Jana on riding."

Alexa had explained Jana's situation so he would know what was going on, and she was thankful she had. Zachary Rutgers had done everything to make Jana feel at home in the saddle, even to the point of having his niece there to help.

When the ranch owner led a huge chestnut toward Alexa, she began to have her doubts about learning to ride. The mare was taller than her, which wasn't that big a deal since she was only five feet two inches. But still, it was a long way to the ground if she fell off. "Do you have a smaller one? Maybe a big pony?"

Zachary chuckled. "Nope. She'll be the best for you. Besides the one Jana is on, this little mare is the gentlest one I have. You'll do fine."

"I bet you say that to all the newbies. Did I mention I've never ridden before?"

"I'm used to teaching greenhorns." He winked and set his black cowboy hat lower on his forehead, shadowing his eyes, before leading the horse out of the barn to a mounting block. "This'll help."

Alexa stepped up on the small wooden platform and searched for Ian. Mounted on an equally large horse, he waited for her by the corral gate, amusement making his eyes sparkle. *Okay, I can do this.*

"Grip the horn, put your left foot in the stirrup and swing your right leg over." Zachary held the reins and the horse still.

Alexa followed his instructions, and a few seconds later sat on top of the mare, staring at how far down the ground really was. Worse than she'd thought.

"Here, take these." Zachary gave her the reins and showed her how to hold them loosely but evenly. "You're in control. Just tell Belle where to go and she will—" he climbed onto his horse and demonstrated for Alexa "—like this."

She could picture herself careening across the field hanging on for dear life. "How do I stop her?"

"This way." He pulled back on the reins. "But not too tight. Their mouths are tender. We'll go slow. This is yours and Jana's first time, so no galloping."

"Thanks. I appreciate that," she squeaked out as he turned his horse and started for the corral where the girls were.

Leaving her behind to figure out how to get Belle to start moving.

Zachary turned in the saddle and said, "Just say go and tap her sides with the heels of your shoes."

He went on outside while Ian waited for her. Belle plodded forward at a sedate pace—thankfully. Alexa's jaw gritted so tightly together, pain streaked down her neck. The squeak of her saddle as she shifted filled her ears.

"You can relax, Alexa," Ian said. "This is supposed to be fun."

"Let me know when the fun starts."

Ian's chuckles peppered the air. "If anyone knows that, it's you. I'll stay right next to you the whole way. Zachary is going to watch over the girls. Ready?"

"Yep," she said, and took a deep breath, then urged Belle forward.

The scent of well-oiled leather and horse wafted to her. After Alexa eased the grip on the reins and started going with the flow of her mare, she scanned the meadow they were crossing to a grove of trees. "This will be beautiful in another month or so."

"Yeah, maybe we'll be doing this again next month." Ian stared at his daughter a few yards ahead of him.

"We all will or at least I will with Jana. Look at that grin on her face. See how she's chatting with Ashley? I read somewhere that riding can make a person feel free, with the wind blowing through their hair, the sun beating down on them. Those are the reasons. Besides, your daughter loves animals. That will bring her back now that she's seen what she's missing."

"Now if only Sugar would come back."

"If for some reason she doesn't, I have confidence you'll find a way to deal with it."

He slowed his horse and looked at her. "I'm glad you do. I wake up some mornings and wonder about what in the world I'm doing. Raising a child, trying to help her through the loss of her mother. Trying to hold my business together but be there for Jana, too."

"You're doing a great job."

He quirked a grin. "Even with all my schedules. I know how you feel about them."

"Because I grew up having to follow one down to the littlest detail."

"Schedules aren't the villain in this."

"No, I'm beginning to see that."

"Ah, so I am rubbing off on you."

Was he? Alexa stared at the gleam in his eyes. She'd

actually stopped by a jewelry counter at the store the other day and considered buying a watch. And just recently, she was thinking of getting a day planner. Oh, my. He was.

As Jana rode toward a grove of trees with Ashley, she glanced over her shoulder at her dad and Alexa. Alexa stared at Jana's father, then laughed at something he said. The expression of joy on his face delighted Jana. She liked Alexa a lot, and she thought her dad did, too.

"Are they dating?" Ashley asked as she peered back in the direction Jana was looking.

"Dating? You mean Alexa and my dad?"

"Yeah."

"No, why do you ask that?"

"They act like they are. You know, like in the movies."

"I think my dad is clueless."

Ashley giggled. "Sounds like my uncle Zachary. At least that's what my mom says. She's thinking of tricking him into dating."

"Tricking him? How?"

"Invite a girl to dinner and him, too. Not make it seem like it's a date but it really is. Throw them together until he gets the picture."

Throw them together? Maybe she could do that. "Alexa is at my house all the time."

"It should be easy then." Ashley snapped her fingers. "I've got a great plan. The HHH Valentine's Day party is next Saturday here at the ranch. Get Alexa to come with you and your dad. You can hang with me and my friends and leave them by themselves."

Maybe if Alexa and her dad started dating, he would be happy all the time. She enjoyed having Alexa around. She could talk to Alexa. Better than she ever did with her mom.

For a few seconds that thought bothered her as though she was a traitor to her own mother, but then she remembered how Alexa was there for her. She made her feel special. Her dad should get to feel that way, too.

Later that afternoon, Alexa finished up helping Jana write a story about her first riding lesson. "Show that to your dad tonight. He'll enjoy it."

"He always enjoys what I write. He's special, don't ya think?"

Alexa started to rise from the kitchen table, but sank back down. Jana's question threw her off balance. "Well, yes, he is."

"He has a good job. He's not bad to look at. He stays in shape, not like some fathers I've seen. He's—"

"What are you doing, Jana?" Finally, Alexa pushed to her feet, looking down at the child, who grinned.

She wiped the smile from her face and shrugged. "Just talking about what a great guy he is." Her mouth formed a pout. "But I think he's lonely. He stays home a lot. He doesn't get to meet nice women like you. He needs to start dating."

"Jana, don't you think you should let your dad make that decision when he's ready?" The thought of Ian dating some other woman didn't sit well with her.

Jana placed her elbow on the table and tapped her finger against her chin. "You know, Ashley said something about the Valentine's party for the families in Helping Hands Homeschooling. I think we should go. What do ya think about doing that?"

"I think that's a great suggestion for you and your dad," Alexa said, all the while thinking: *Jana's trying to fix her dad up with other women.* Her stomach roiled as though she'd eaten something that didn't agree with her.

"Great. It's next Saturday night. Put it on your calendar. We're gonna have fun."

"But I didn't mean me. It's a family affair."

"You've got to come. I won't know too many people there." Jana's pout strengthened. "Maybe I shouldn't go."

Alexa put her hand on her waist. "Jana Ferguson, you're manipulating me."

"Is it working? Will ya go?"

"Fine, I'll be there on Saturday night." Alexa shoved in her chair, started to turn toward the kitchen to refill her mug, when she stopped. "Where is the Valentine's Day party?" She wasn't agreeing because of Ian but because of Jana. The more the child got out of the house, the better it would be for Jana.

Yeah, right, Alexa.

Okay, Ian needs someone to save him from getting involved with the wrong woman.

Oh, that's a good one.

"The party's at the ranch in the barn. Won't that be different? Ashley told me there would be square dancing. Her uncle learned to call it while they were doing a unit on the Old West."

"Square dancing? I've never done it."

Jana rose and leaned close to Alexa. "Tell ya a secret, neither has Dad. In fact, I don't think Dad has ever danced. He said something about having two left feet once when he came in while I was watching a show about dancing on TV. You ought to get him out on the dance floor. You two should be a riot."

The flush of embarrassment heated Alexa's cheeks. "I don't think I want to be the object of amusement for anyone. And I'm sure your dad doesn't either."

"I'm just kidding. Zachary is gonna teach some of the

steps so people can do it. I hope you can get Dad to dance. He needs to have some fun again."

"You'd have a better chance than me." Alexa covered the distance to the kitchen and picked up the kettle from the stove to pour some hot water for her tea. "Don't you have a birthday coming up soon?" she asked, hoping to take Jana off the topic of her father.

"Yeah, March 8th."

"What are you gonna do for it?"

Jana lifted her shoulders, her arms out wide. "Any suggestions?"

"A party. Invite your friends."

"Other than Ashley I've lost track of most of them this past year."

"Well, you've got the kids that come to class on Wednesdays and Fridays. Then there are Kelly and Aaron next door. Think about it. Maybe it would be a good time to see how your old friends are doing. Or you could have a slumber party with a few girls. Watch movies, eat lots of popcorn and stay up all night."

Jana's eyes grew round as Alexa ticked off activities the kids could do. "I like that!"

"Like what, pumpkin?" Ian asked from the doorway, his hair a bit tousled, the long sleeves on his white shirt rolled up.

Alexa paused in stirring the sugar into her tea. *He looks good.* The thought stopped her movements and sent her heart beating double time.

"Alexa thinks I should have a party for my birthday."

"She does?" Ian's penetratingly blue gaze latched on to hers. "I suppose you're going to volunteer to chaperone, too."

Alexa brought the mug to her lips and took a tentative sip. "Jana hasn't decided what she's gonna do."

"Yes, I have. I want to have a sleepover the Friday night before, and you being here to keep my dad in line is great."

No way in a thousand years. In fact, never. Too dangerous to my peace of mind. "I'll have to check my calendar. I seem to remember my singles group at church has something going on." Which was true. They did the first Friday of every month, and she had attended a few times when work and schooling permitted. *Maybe I can come up with something more interesting than a slumber party for a soon-to-be eleven-year-old.*

"You've got to be there. I wouldn't be having one if you hadn't said anything."

Thanks for reminding me of that one. When am I going to really think things through before saying anything? "Let me see, but that shouldn't stop you from making plans with your dad." Alexa shot Ian a look. "And I can help with any planning and shopping for food. Actually, Jana, that would be good for us to do together."

For a moment Jana's teeth worried her bottom lip. "Will ya come for a part of the night at least if I do?"

"Ah, manipulating me twice in less than half an hour." Alexa crossed to the window that afforded her a view of the lake and swept around to face the pair. "Fine. I'll come and stay until midnight. Then, Ian, you're on your own."

Jana clapped. "Perfect. I'm gonna get some paper and make a list of who I'm gonna invite."

The second she left the kitchen Alexa held up her hand. "Don't say anything. I spoke before I really thought about it. I'm sorry…"

His strides chewed up the distance between them. "Do you realize what you've done?"

She nodded. "But I'm not really sure you fully realize."

He came to a halt a foot from her. "I'm almost afraid to ask what."

A lump welled in her throat, not from anything he said, but from his nearness. "No sleep, loud noises, total disruption in any schedule you've got. Should I go on?" she asked over the drumming beat of her heart in her ears.

"Please, no. I think ignorance in this case might be bliss." Cutting the space between them even more, he bent forward. "Today was great. It's something I'd hoped would happen for quite some time, and now, for her to be reaching out to friends and wanting to spend time with them—it's wonderful. Well worth any amount of loud noise."

His musky scent engulfed her, her pulse rate responding to it. Ever since Sunday when he'd almost kissed her, she'd wondered what it would be like. Dreamed about it. Then today, Jana's attempts at matchmaking had rekindled the hope yet again. Even though there were so many reasons she should back away, put the length of the room between them, she stayed rooted to the floor, praying her longing wasn't visible in her eyes.

He took her face between his hands, his fingertips roughened and warm to the touch. "Jana was happy, content while at the ranch, and you're the reason it happened. When you first came here, I didn't think it would work out. Your teaching methods are—" he paused, as though searching for the right word "—so different from what is traditional. Since then I've discovered there are many ways for a child to learn and not to confine myself to just one."

She noticed he'd loosened up some while teaching his math class on Wednesdays and Fridays. But she also realized simply going with the flow wasn't totally right either. She and Jana had a routine they followed because the girl needed to know what came next.

He inched closer. "Thank you for taking the job and going beyond what a tutor does."

The feel of his hands on her face branded her as if in that moment she'd become his. The realization struck terror in her, and yet she couldn't move away. She remembered the pain of Daniel's loss. Never wanted to experience it again. And she'd spent weeks telling herself that she and Ian were just too different. But she remained frozen as Ian lowered his head toward hers.

His half-lidded survey of her roamed a leisurely path from her hair to her eyes to her lips. More inches that separated them disappeared. The scent of his peppermint toothpaste swirled about her, roping her to him.

She wanted him to kiss her. Badly.

The soft brush of his lips tingled down her length. She wanted more.

The thundering in her ears evolved into honking and barking. She blinked, wrenched from the moment as Ian lifted his head slightly and looked beyond her out the window.

His eyes grew round. "Well, I'll be."

"What?" She whirled around and stared at the scene outside near the lake.

Four geese surrounded Sugar. The largest male went in for a nip. The dog spun around and barked some more.

Ian flew toward the door.

Pushing away all thoughts of the too-brief kiss, Alexa hurried after him, shouting, "Jana, come quick. Sugar's out back."

Ian gestured toward the right. "You go that way. I'll go this way." Veering to the left, he increased his jog, waving his arms and saying, "Scat."

The big male goose peered at Ian as though he were crazy, which, when Alexa thought about it, was what he looked like. The gander honked and hissed, charging at Ian. The other male followed suit while the two females waddled back into the water.

Ian kept moving forward. "Get Sugar while I distract them."

Alexa slowed her pace so she didn't scare the dog. Sugar sat and continued to yelp in a high-pitched tone, her leash still attached to the pet.

"That's it. Stay right there, Sugar," she said in a soothing voice while a battle raged a few yards from her.

One gander nipped Ian on the leg, then the other one did. Ian backed away, flailing his arms like a windmill.

Alexa grabbed the end of the leash then scooped Sugar up into her embrace and hung on for dear life. The back door banged close, and Jana raced toward them, brandishing the sweater Alexa had worn to work.

The largest gander took a look at the third human invading his territory, gave one final hiss and padded back to the lake, with the other male trailing behind him. Quickly the four geese swam away.

"Are you all right?" Alexa asked Ian while she handed the dog to Jana, and the child passed her the sweater.

"I think my pride is all that's hurt." Massaging his thigh, Ian checked on the geese's progress out to the middle of the lake. "Those two ganders could give lessons to the military on defending their territory. Hon, is Sugar okay?" he asked his daughter.

"She's great. She came home." Jana hugged her dog to her chest. "I'm never letting her go." She started for the house, rubbing her face against Sugar's neck, the leash dragging on the ground behind them.

"Life may get interesting around the Ferguson household with my daughter lugging her dog everywhere she goes." Limping slightly, Ian headed for the patio.

"She'll get tired of it after a while. Fifteen pounds doesn't sound like a lot until you carry it a long time." Alexa glanced at the time on the clock in the kitchen. "I've got to go. My class starts in twenty minutes."

"You wouldn't have been so surprised if you had a watch on and kept track of the time."

His grin that accompanied that observation made her frown. "You enjoyed pointing that out." She wouldn't even go into the fact that earlier, her lack of attention to the time had more to do with him briefly kissing her, not her lack of a watch. He could distract more than a gaggle of geese honking at the same time.

At school, Dr. Baker stopped Alexa right after her class. "How's it going with Jana and Ian?"

"Fine. Jana is doing great. She struggles with math, but we've been doing some hands-on activities that I think have helped."

"I've heard from one or two of the kids who come over for math lessons that they're doing some fun projects after Mr. Ferguson explains the concept. Is that your doing?"

"Not for the past week. Ian's getting into it and has been coming up with different ways to help the kids with fractions. Next he's gonna do some geometry with them. That should be interesting."

"Has Sugar been found?" Nancy started walking toward the main foyer.

"Yes. Right before I came to class."

"Good, I'm glad Sugar is home where she belongs." She glanced at Alexa. "I've been wanting to talk to you. I've found a scholarship I want you to apply for. It's a full scholarship for a year, which includes tuition, books, and living expenses for two semesters, plus it will pay off your student loans in exchange for committing to teaching for three years in an underdeveloped country where Christian Teachers International runs a school. You could complete your schooling by December instead of the summer semester next year. I know you've dreamed of working overseas, and I know you've got some hefty student loans. This could be your opportunity. Come to my office. I'll give you the paperwork."

Alexa paused in the large entrance area into the Education Building. "When is the deadline?"

"Three weeks. The organization will interview the four finalists in Oklahoma City, and if you get it, you could go full-time this summer and finish up with student teaching in the fall and a few classes. What do you say?"

Nancy dangled her dream before her, but for a moment all she could think about was Jana's look of joy when she'd seen Sugar and Ian's expression as he'd cupped her face right before his lips had touched hers. She wouldn't see them after she left Tallgrass if she got the scholarship, at least not for three years. Yet this was what she and Daniel had wanted to do. She'd promised him at his memorial service to fulfill their dream.

"Alexa, is everything all right?"

She shook the thoughts from her mind. "Yes. You're right, this is an opportunity I can't pass up."

Nancy moved across the foyer toward the hallway where the faculty offices were. "If you're the winner, you'll know by the second week in April."

"I've got to fill out the application and be one of the finalists first."

Inside her office, Nancy crossed to her desk, rummaged

through a stack of folders and pulled one out. "Here's the application. It'll take a few hours to complete, but it'll be well worth it. Christian Teachers International has some dynamite people working for them."

The small pile of papers in the folder attested to the hours she would have to invest. "Thanks, Nancy. I appreciate you thinking of me."

"You're the only one of my students I thought had a chance at this scholarship. See you Thursday."

Out in the hallway Alexa flipped through the pages in the folder. This was her future—not anyone here in Tallgrass. She stuck the application in her backpack then hurried toward her car. She'd start answering the questions tonight and would work each night until the paperwork was completed.

But when she pulled into her driveway at the duplex, she noticed a vehicle parked behind her mother's. A black Lincoln Town Car. One of Mom's new friends? She'd say hello to whoever it was and then quickly escape to her bedroom to work on her application.

When she opened the door to her place, she heard low, intense voices coming from the kitchen. One was a deep bass. A male? Her mom was seeing a man? Cautiously she tiptoed toward her bedroom, deciding to disappear without telling her mother she was home.

Halfway down the short hall, her mom said, "Alexa, your dad is here in the kitchen."

Chapter Eight

"Dad? Here?" Alexa clutched her backpack. *No! Not here. Not now.*

Her mother nodded.

"Why didn't you tell me he was coming?"

"Because I didn't know. He surprised me."

Alexa stepped closer to her mother and lowered her voice. "Where's he staying?"

"I'm staying at Tallgrass Inn, at least for the night."

Alexa stiffened, but the fingers holding her book bag went slack and it fell to the floor. The thud echoed down the hallway. Her gaze swept to him standing at the end of the corridor, only three feet away. She wanted to cross the distance and hug him—the way Jana did Ian, but the hard look in his eyes, the firm set of his shoulders, the balled hands at his sides proclaimed his anger. She stayed put, remembering all the times she'd wanted to be accepted unconditionally by him but never felt she had been.

"I'll be back tomorrow morning to resume our conversation, Gloria." Dr. Richard Michaels pivoted and traversed the small entryway to the front door. "Good night."

Alexa slowly blew a long breath out when the click sounded, announcing his exit. "When did he come?"

"He was only here an hour."

"And?" Alexa bent and picked up her backpack, her hand trembling badly as she grasped the bag to her chest, crisscrossing her arms around it.

"There's nothing to tell. I listened to him tell me I should come home. That I'd been gone long enough. Right before you came home he asked if I'd gotten my rebellion out of my system yet."

Alexa clenched her teeth together. It wasn't her place to say anything to her mother. She didn't want to get into the middle of a fight between her parents. "Are you gonna see him tomorrow?"

"Since he came six hundred miles to see me, I at least owe him that, but he isn't going to change my mind. I was smothering living under his roof. Did I tell you at the end of last week I applied for a part-time job at the hospital?"

"No, how did you forget something like that?"

"Because I didn't want to say anything to you unless I got the position. They called me early this afternoon. After I talk with your father tomorrow morning, I have an appointment about my new job."

"Congratulations—I think. Are you sure this is what you want?"

"I know what I don't want. I don't want to be a wife to a man who doesn't appreciate me. I don't want to be defined as Dr. Michaels's wife. I want something that is mine." Her mother took her hand. "You're cold. Are you all right?"

"I don't know what to think, Mom. I guess I'm numb more than anything. Since I had eighteen years to learn how to deal with it, I should be able to accept by now that there are no warm fuzzies for me from my father, even after not seeing me for five years."

"I'm so sorry, honey. That's why I want you to be very careful with your feelings concerning Ian. He keeps his emotions bottled up inside him just like your father."

Not toward his daughter.

"You think you're going to be able to change someone, but you can't change a person. They are the only ones who can change themselves. When I married your father, I thought he would learn to open up to me. He never did."

"You don't have to worry about me. I have no illusions about Ian." Alexa unzipped her backpack. "Besides, Nancy gave me a scholarship application today that if I'm picked will help me fulfill one of my dreams, teaching in an under-developed country where I'm needed." After removing the folder, she passed it to her mother. "I'll get to see some of the world and help others while I teach. What could be better?"

Having a family came unbidden into her mind. She quickly closed the door on that train of thought.

"I know how much working and going to school has been a struggle for you, Alexa. If this is what you want, I'll pray it happens for you." Her mother returned the application to her.

She hugged her mom and kissed her on the cheek. "I love you and will be behind you whatever you decide."

Gloria cupped her cheek, tears glistening in her eyes. "Thanks, honey. Now I better get a good night's sleep. I have a lot to do tomorrow, not to mention I have to face your father."

As her mother disappeared inside her bedroom, Alexa ran her fingers over the place where her mother had touched her face. Just as Ian had earlier. The memory—so vivid it seemed as though she felt his caress all over again—mocked her decision to pursue her dream.

* * *

"I need to go, Mom. I'm running late." After grabbing a piece of toast and her mug of tea, Alexa headed for the front door.

"Bye, dear."

Alexa threw a glance back at her mother sitting at the kitchen table, cupping her drink between her hands while she stared at the empty chair across from her. Alexa swung around in the entrance. "I'll be praying for you."

"And your father."

Alexa continued her trek toward the foyer. Her mixed feelings toward her dad had kept her up a good part of the night. Hence the reason she was running late. She hadn't fallen asleep until around four.

When she hurried out onto the porch, she came to a halt. Her father was mounting the steps, his gaze locked on her. He was early. She'd wanted to be gone before he arrived. As she studied his face, she noticed the lines around his eyes, mouth and forehead were deeper. His thick, black hair was thinning on top, and his bright brown eyes were dull. And for the first time she could see a pouch where his stomach had always been flat from years of running and keeping in shape. Her father had aged more than five years and the observation held her rooted to the spot.

He closed the space between them, his gaze never leaving her face. "You're looking well."

The words were spoken as though she were a casual acquaintance. Not his daughter. No warmth behind them. No love. Her heart cracked anew and the tears she'd held back last night jammed her throat, prodding her to release them. She wouldn't cry in front of him ever again. She'd cried a lifetime's worth five years ago. Not now.

"I'm doing what I love. I'm glad it shows," Alexa said,

refusing to squirm under the relentless stare probing for some weakness.

"It does. But you would have made a wonderful doctor. I always dreamed of you taking over my practice one day."

Like a son would? The thought that he'd probably wanted another son to replace the one he'd lost, but had to settle for her, inundated her. "Not if I couldn't stomach the sight of blood. I think that would have interfered in doing my job."

For a second the old sparkle that usually lit his eyes flashed, only to disappear before taking hold. "Yeah, that's an inconvenience, but it's not too late to change your mind. If you set your heart on something, you can do anything."

"That was the problem. My heart wasn't ever set on being a doctor." She lifted her chin. "And whether you approve or not, I've gotten where I am totally by myself and I'm doing just fine. Now, if you'll excuse me, I have a job I have to go to." She descended the first step.

"Alexa, I'd like to take you to lunch today. Are you available?"

At the bottom of the stairs she looked up at him, standing tall, commanding, demanding. "Why?"

"Because I haven't seen you in five years."

The denial was on the tip of her tongue. She wanted to say it. But couldn't. "I don't know," she finally answered, her stomach churning, sweat popping out on her upper lip.

"Check with your employer and give me a call. I'll be here with your mother."

No "I've missed you." No "I love you." She spun on her heel and marched toward her car. How many times had she wanted to hear him tell her he loved her over the years until she'd finally resigned herself to the fact he wouldn't? Now he'd come in and opened all those healed wounds.

* * *

Alexa paused in the entrance to Ian's office. "I know Madge is here and can keep an eye on Jana, but I wanted to let you know I'm leaving for lunch with my father. I shouldn't be gone more than an hour. Are you okay with this?"

Ian smiled. "All the extra time you've spent here, I'm more than fine with it. If you need longer, take it. I'll make sure Jana does the schoolwork you've left her."

"I won't be more than an hour."

Ian's forehead creased. "Is something wrong?"

"I don't want to meet with my father. I'm not looking forward to this. I can't imagine we'll have much to talk about."

"Does he still want you to be a doctor?"

She nodded.

"I'd love for Jana to be a CPA like me. It's a good job, and she'll be able to make a good living doing it, but I've given up on that. Numbers and Jana don't get along. I've accepted that, but it won't stop me from trying to guide her toward a stable career."

"Guide and insist are two different things."

"Maybe he just wants to talk about your mother."

"Maybe. I'd better go. I'm meeting him at the restaurant at Tallgrass Inn."

Alexa left Ian's house and rushed toward her car. She'd just have enough time to get to the restaurant if the traffic cooperated. She turned the key in the ignition. Nothing. Not even a grinding sound like she'd had once before. Dead. She laid her head against the steering wheel and closed her eyes.

What do I do? I don't have Dad's cell number. Mom's at her meeting at the hospital. She had to go in and call the inn. A phone call she dreaded.

She climbed from her car, covered the distance to the house and rang the bell. Ian opened the front door half a minute later.

"My car's dead."

"Probably the battery. I could give you a jump, and you could go to a store and get it replaced."

"I don't have time to deal with that. I can call my cousin, and he'll come take care of it later." Her left thumb kneaded her right palm. "I've got to get a taxi and get to the restaurant *now*." Her voice rose with a frantic ring to the words. Being on time had always been important to her dad, and she had disappointed him on a number of occasions.

"Then let me take you to meet your father. I have some errands that I was going to do later. I'll just do them now."

"You don't mind changing your plans?" She eased up rubbing a sore spot in the middle of her hand.

"I know a young lady who told me I need to be more flexible. No, I don't mind. Let me go tell Madge and Jana where I'm going."

"Thank you."

Alexa paced the length of the porch while she waited. She'd psyched herself up for this meeting, and she wanted to get it over with. She'd meet with her dad then she could go on about what she was doing with no regrets. The rest was in the Lord's hands.

"Ready?" Ian closed the front door.

"Yes," she said as though she were preparing to stand before a firing squad.

Ten minutes later and five minutes late, Alexa opened Ian's car door and exited.

"I'll be back here at one. Okay?" Ian sent her a smile. "You'll do fine. If he didn't care about you, he wouldn't have asked to meet with you today."

Alexa walked toward the inn, Ian's last statement replaying in her mind. That simply wasn't true. Her father had never shown her the kind of love that Ian showed his daughter every day. The way her dad dealt with people was to order and control. It had nothing to do with caring about them.

Standing in the entrance into the restaurant, she scanned the patrons and found her father seated along the wall at a table for two. A frown marked the lines on his face and emphasized the type of hour she would have. Tension bubbled in her stomach, making any thought of eating nearly impossible.

When she appeared at his side, he looked up, and his frown dissolved. Her eyes widened at the sight as his mouth tilted up in a half grin.

"I thought you were going to stand me up." He gestured toward the chair across from him. "Sit and let's order."

"I'm not hungry. I'll just have a cup of tea." *Something that will calm my nerves.*

"Fine." He waved for the waitress, and when she came over to the table, they gave her their orders.

After the young woman left, her father asked, "Are you feeling all right?"

"I'm okay. Just not…" She wasn't going to do it—sit here and act as if they had a normal father/daughter relationship where pleasantries were exchanged and all was well with the world. It wasn't. "To tell you the truth, my stomach is in knots because I haven't been looking forward to this lunch."

"I see."

"Do you? You kicked me out of the house and told me if I didn't do what you wanted not to come back." Now that the dam on her anger had cracked—the way her heart had all these years ago—she couldn't stop herself. "Why do you want to talk to me?"

He blinked rapidly, averted his gaze for a long moment, then fastened it back on her face, a softening in his expression for a few seconds before it gelled into its usual sober expression. "I wanted your help with your mother. I wanted you to help me make her see what a mistake she's making."

"Ah. Now I understand." She clutched the edge of the table and leaned forward. "If she wants a job, what's the harm? People have to live their own lives." She realized she wasn't just talking about her mother anymore.

"And throw away twenty-five years?"

"Why can't you let her be herself?" She couldn't stay. She couldn't pretend this wasn't also about her, too. Bolting to her feet, she stared down at him, his expression unreadable. She searched his dark eyes and saw no love in their depths. She saw nothing. "I can't do this. You'll have to work it out with Mom. Don't drag me into the middle." She'd said more than she'd ever intended.

She turned to leave.

"Alexa, I need your help."

She glanced back, and for the briefest moment she glimpsed hurt before he quickly masked it. "I can't."

With hurried steps she moved toward the exit, seeking only to escape before she released the tears that clogged her throat, choking off any decent breath. Her lungs burned from the lack of oxygen. At the restaurant entrance she chanced a look back and found her father weaving his way through the crowded tables toward her.

Please, Lord, I can't handle this. Help me.

Just short of running, she made it outside. The welcoming cold of the air bathed her hot cheeks. She looked up and down the street, trying to find a place to hide until Ian showed up. When she saw his car parked in the lot beside the inn, she trembled with relief as she rushed toward Ian's vehicle.

When she climbed into his white sedan, she asked, "Can you leave right now?"

"Are you okay?"

Her father stopped at the edge of the parking lot and stared right at her. She twisted toward Ian. "No, I can't talk with him right now."

Ian started the car and pulled out of the space, avoiding the area where her father still stood, watching her.

After her dad disappeared from her view, she relaxed against the cushion, flexing her hands to ease the tension from fisting them. "Why didn't you run your errands?" *Was that my voice that shook?*

"I did one then I just had this feeling I needed to come back to the inn and wait for you."

"I'm glad. I didn't want to have that conversation on Main Street."

"What conversation?" Ian slid her a glance, full of compassion.

That look unleashed the emotions bottled up for years— ones she hadn't even been able to say to her father. "Why doesn't he love me? What did I do wrong?" Tears leaked down her face, and she tried to brush them away but more instantly replaced them. "I tried all my life to please him until I couldn't do it anymore."

Ian turned into a nearly deserted parking lot and stopped the car away from any nearby people. Twisting toward her, he settled his arm along the back cushion. "Is that when you left home?"

She nodded, the lump in her throat so huge she didn't think she could say anything. And the tears still flowed from her as a turmoil of feelings—worthlessness, guilt, sadness that she'd kept suppressed—flooded her.

Ian drew her to him, encircling her with his warm, protective embrace that conveyed support, that he cared about her.

She sobbed against his shirt, wishing she had been able to change what had happened, wishing she knew why she wasn't worthy of her father's love. Slowly she focused on the feel of Ian's hand as it stroked the length of her back over and over.

She finally heard his soothing words, "It's okay, Alexa. Let it all go."

Embarrassment washed over her, her wet-streaked cheeks flushed with heat. She'd never intended to fall apart in his presence. She pulled back, wiping her hand across her face. "I'm sorry. I don't know what overcame me."

"Your father hurt you. You can't keep that inside forever."

For a flash she got a peek at Ian's own hurt, caused by his wife. She wanted to know so much more about the man who held her while she cried about all the regrets of her childhood. Not once had her father held her and let her cry because she was hurting.

"You want to talk about it? It might help."

The earnest appeal in his blue eyes unraveled her newly pulled-together composure. The tears threatened again as she looked at him. No more! She couldn't change what happened and no amount of crying would rewrite her past. She swallowed several times. "All my life my father demanded I do things his way, saying that he knew what was best for me. What subjects I should take in school. What extracurricular activities I would do. For the record, I hated piano lessons and had to endure them for ten years. I wanted to do debate. He thought I should be in the science club and concentrate on that because he wanted me to become a doctor. There were times I didn't feel like I was living my life but his."

"There are some parents who don't care enough what their children are doing. At least he wasn't that way."

"But I was miserable. And even when I did what he'd ordered, whatever I did wasn't good enough for him. He wanted me to do even better. I can't remember him telling me he loved me. I needed to hear that. I needed to hear occasionally I was doing a good job."

"Did you ever tell him how you felt?" Ian kneaded his hand into her shoulder, easing the tension gripping her.

"I didn't dare until that last year at home. After Daniel died unexpectedly, my life fell apart. Daniel and I had planned to marry after a year or so at college. I needed my father to love me. Instead, all he did was tell me his plans for my future. If it hadn't been for my mother, I don't know what would have happened. I felt myself coming apart. Finally I graduated, and a month later I left."

"What did he say?"

"I wrote him a note. I did tell Mom right before. I didn't want her to worry about me, but I couldn't face him with what I was going to do. I got in the car and drove until I ended up here. I had some cousins who lived here, and it looked like a nice place to live and go to college." The feel of his fingers massaging her tight muscles made her relax back against the cushion, close her eyes for a moment and savor the bond between them.

"What did he say when you finally talked with him?"

"That he couldn't support my decision, and that I was a disappointment to him. Up until he appeared in Tallgrass, I hadn't seen him in five years."

"Have you ever looked at this situation from his viewpoint?"

Alexa drew back against the passenger door. "His viewpoint. What is it?"

"Everyone has his side to the story. I'm not condoning his behavior. I'm just saying, have you asked him about why he did what he did?" Ian faced forward, gripping the steering wheel. "I'm a father, and some of his actions I can certainly understand. I want the best for my daughter. I will try my best to guide her toward what I think is best."

"The key word here is *guide,* not *dictate.*"

"True. But maybe your dad doesn't know any other way than to demand."

"And that's supposed to make it right?"

"All I'm saying is you need to have that conversation with your father. Hear his side. You tell him yours. Do you want to live the rest of your life wondering, angry, hurting?"

"No." Would listening to her dad bring some kind of closure on her childhood? Would it help her to forgive him? She knew that was what the Lord wanted her to do. She just didn't know if she could.

Ian started the car. "Pick a private place. A restaurant or the street isn't a place to have that conversation." As he backed out of the parking space, he peered at her. "And I'll be here to listen afterward."

Another brick around her defenses crumbled at his offer. Every time she was with him she discovered more things to like about Ian—someone a month ago she would have said was night to her day. Yes, they were still very different, and yet there was a connection to him she hadn't experienced since Daniel. The realization scared her.

"So you're gonna come pick me up for church tomorrow?" Jana asked from the backseat of Ian's car.

Alexa angled toward her. "If it's okay with your dad."

"Can I, Dad? I want to go to church with Alexa."

Ian parked in front of the corral at the Wild Bill Buffalo Ranch. "Will you be okay if I don't go? I have a lot of work I need to get done."

Doubt clouding her eyes, Jana glanced from her father to Alexa. "Are ya sure ya can't come?"

"Hon, not tomorrow. I've gotten behind and need the time to catch up."

Jana squared her shoulders. "I'll be all right then, but I hope you'll come next week."

"Next week?" One of his eyebrows arched. "Planning ahead. Has Alexa agreed?"

"Well, no." Her brow creased, Jana swung her attention to Alexa.

"You can go anytime I go." *But I hope your dad will come, too.*

"Great. Let's get a move on it. The party has started." Jana climbed from the car and rushed toward Ashley, who stood in the barn entrance.

"Have you square-danced before?" Ian opened his door and the light brightened the interior, illuminating the hesitation in his expression.

"No. Have you?"

"Nope. And whenever I danced in the past, I've had two left feet, so I'm warning you now."

For just a moment Alexa felt as though they were on a date. Which wasn't the case. She had to remember that. She was here because of Jana—not Ian. And yet she had gotten ready as if she was going on a date. Even the fact Ian had picked her up at her house, and come to her door had re-inforced that feeling.

"Well, I'm pretty coordinated, so I'll help you make it through the evening." Alexa exited the car, the cool night air enveloping her. She shivered. She should have worn more than a sweater.

"Cold?"

"It's a little chillier than I thought it would be. You just never know in Oklahoma about the weather, especially in February. Sunny and seventy degrees one day and snowing the next."

He removed his jacket. "Here, wear this. The cold doesn't usually bother me. I have a feeling when we get inside it'll be warm. Look at all the people attending." After gesturing at the vehicles parked near the barn, he slipped his coat over her shoulders.

She snuggled into its warmth, his male scent wrapping around her. Her pulse picked up speed as though his arms had surrounded her in a hug. What would it be like if he kissed her? Not a brush of his lips across hers. Something much more than that. "You're probably right. Did everyone in the HHH group show up here?"

"I know at the meeting last week the kids were looking forward to it and so were the parents."

"Jana told me she finally went with you to a meeting and had a good time."

"I think her friendship with Ashley is helping draw her into the activities. That and your influence."

"I wish my class wasn't on the night you meet with the other parents. I'd love to attend one. Maybe during spring break next month. I'll have the week off."

"If you've got your planner, pencil us in. How's it working for you?" Ian paused in the entrance to the barn.

"If I would look at it each morning, it would work better. Just writing an activity on the calendar doesn't mean anything if I don't check it the day it's supposed to happen. I'm not used to having a planner, so I've missed a few things." Scanning the crowd, she saw a few familiar faces. "I see Nancy. I'm gonna go say hi."

Before she took a step away, Ian snagged her hand. "When the dancing starts, don't leave me stranded."

Her heart fluttered. The appeal in his eyes accelerated her pulse rate even more. "I'm sure Jana would be your partner."

"She said she hopes Randy asks her to dance. She all but told me to stay away and give him a chance. I know she'll be eleven in a few weeks, but she's growing up too fast. She's beginning to think about boys."

Alexa leaned close to Ian. "I have news for you. She probably was thinking about boys before now."

His eyes grew huge. "This is the part about being a father I'm fearing."

She patted his arm. "You'll do fine. I won't abandon you when Zachary gets started with the square dancing."

As she walked toward Nancy off to the side by the refreshment table, she couldn't help wondering if her father had feared the same thing. She'd never given him much reason to because when she was sixteen, she'd begun dating Daniel, the son of close friends to her parents. He'd often been at her house as though he were part of the family.

She greeted her adviser with a smile. "You all did a great job on the decorations." Her gaze roamed over the Western-style Valentine's Day theme—hearts done in a red-and-white checker pattern, small Stetsons filled with red-and-white, heart-shaped candy, a cut-out poster of a woman being roped by a cowboy who was pulling her toward him.

"Ashley's family and a couple of other people did all this. I can't take credit for it." Nancy stepped away from the table off to the side, where it wasn't crowded. "I'm glad to see you here with Jana and Ian. You've been so good for her. When I saw them at the meeting this last week, Ian stopped to tell me thanks for recommending you."

"He did?" She searched the throng and found Ian standing with Zachary, talking. In his quiet way Ian commanded a person's attention. Dressed in jeans, a plaid shirt and boots, he looked as much a cowboy as Zachary. Although Ian wasn't used to this casual attire, the only thing, however, that gave him away was the brand-new boots that stuck out from his slightly worn jeans.

"Yes." Nancy studied her a moment. "I've noticed lately in class you've been distracted. It's not like you to be lost in thought. Is everything all right?"

"My dad is still here. I thought he would go back by now."

"Isn't that good? Aren't you glad they're trying to work out their issues?"

"You know about my issues with my father." Not long after saying something to Ian, she'd also confided to Nancy about what was going on with her and her father. "Ian thinks I need to have that conversation with my father. I don't know if I can. I've been avoiding him since we met for lunch, but it's getting hard. He's always at the house when my mom is there. He's determined to get Mom to come home with him. And when my father is determined, nothing stands in his way."

"But you did." Nancy shifted farther away from the crowd.

"Yeah, which is probably why he wants to talk. To try one more time to get me to do what he wants."

"Do you know that for sure?"

"I know my dad. He hasn't changed. He's pressing my mom hard to return home."

"I think Ian is right. Talk to him. Try to forgive him, Alexa. That's the only way you'll be free to move on. As long as you hold your anger inside, you'll never be totally free from your father."

"I know." But the thought of that conversation chilled her blood.

After observing his daughter learn the DoSaDo step then the flutterwheel—where in the world did they come up with these names for dance steps—Ian had his doubts about not making a fool of himself. Maybe if he disappeared in the crowd of people in a circle around the floor set up in the barn for the square dancing, Jana would forget he was here. Then he remembered her challenge as she'd come off the floor with Randy with the biggest grin on her face. She didn't think he could do it. He rubbed the taut muscles along the back of his neck. The problem was, he didn't know if he could do it either.

Alexa appeared at his side. He sensed her before he glanced at her.

Her smile twinkled in her eyes. "Are you ready?"

"No, let's go for a walk. Maybe some fresh air will help."

"With what?"

"My coordination. My…" He shrugged. "Okay. I don't like being onstage. There, I said it. My big secret is out."

She chuckled. "I used to feel that way. But since I'm studying to be a teacher, I had to overcome it. Teachers are 'onstage' every day."

"So it doesn't bother you to get up in front of fifty people and do something you don't know how to do?"

"Are these people friends?"

"Yeah."

"Then you should be all right." She pointed to the couples heading out into the center. "I'm sure we won't be the only novices out there."

After fifteen minutes of instruction, Ian wasn't so sure he wasn't the only novice attempting to square-dance. Even Alexa looked like a pro compared to him. He tried another run at the Chain Down the Line step and ended up spinning Alexa in the wrong direction, which caused him to face the man across from him instead of the woman.

"Okay, let's try that again," Zachary said as he walked over to Ian and stood by him. When he began the call, he guided Ian in the right direction.

"I think I've got it now." After Zachary left, Ian whispered, "I think he's speaking a foreign language."

"You're doing great."

"Yeah, if they allowed an elephant to do it. I'm sorry I stepped on your foot. At least you aren't limping anymore."

"Okay, we're gonna try this to a song. Ready." Zachary signaled the person running the sound system to cue up the song.

Ian completed the first move behind the others, and the rest of the song went downhill from there. By the time he promenaded Alexa down the middle, his cheeks felt like they were on fire. But he stuck with it to the very last note. The audience erupted into applause. Ian made a direct line to the fringe of the crowd surrounding the dance floor, practically dragging Alexa with him. He dived through the throng and kept striding toward the exit.

Outside in the cooler night air, he faced Alexa. "Did I do as bad a job as I think?"

The lights from inside illuminated her expression, not one sign of ridicule in it. "You did fine. You might not have noticed the others made mistakes, but everyone did. Square dancing isn't something you do effortlessly overnight. I can tell you, your daughter was clapping louder than anyone there."

"She was?"

"Yep."

"I felt out of control on the dance floor."

"You don't like being out of control?"

"Does anyone?"

"True, probably not. But I learned I'm really not in control. Once I accepted that the Lord had the final say, I let a lot go."

"So you've never felt like your life is falling apart around you?"

"Yes." She averted her gaze, staring off into space. "When Daniel died unexpectedly my life came completely apart right after that. All the plans I'd made with him were gone. I didn't know what to do. All I knew was I didn't want to go to medical school like my father wanted. Instead of staying and making my dad see my side, I fled. Now I'm beginning to wonder if that was the best way to have handled the situation. I knew my dad would be angry and make demands I wouldn't fulfill. I think secretly I was hoping that would happen. Then the hard decisions would be taken away from me."

Was she still in love with Daniel? That thought gave him pause. There was a time he'd loved Tracy, but she'd crushed that love. Her betrayal had hurt him. Alexa also had, in a way, been hurt by someone who had abandoned her. Was that why he felt a connection with her? Their bond scared him. And yet, he couldn't seem to resist it.

Ian took her hands and tugged her away from the entrance and a couple leaving the barn. Positioning himself against the railing of the corral, he drew her close. "What decisions?"

"What do I really want in life? How do I go about getting it? Why do I want whatever it is? What is my purpose? I reacted without thought to Dad, and I haven't stopped to really answer those questions."

"I thought you wanted to be a teacher." His thumb rubbed a circle in her palm, the tingling sensations of their touch robbing him of coherent thought for a few seconds. He considered releasing her hands but didn't want to break the physical connection.

"Yes, but what do I want to do with that? Do I still want to travel the world and teach in underdeveloped countries like Daniel and I talked about? It was his dream as much as mine. I latched on to it and escaped to Tallgrass to fulfill it."

"Do you still want to do it?"

"I'm applying for a scholarship Nancy told me about. If I get it, I'll be going to school full-time and finishing my degree two semesters early. Then I'll be placed for three years in a third world country through the group that sponsored the scholarship. This is an opportunity I've been dreaming about for years and only lately have I realized it is my dream as much as it was Daniel's."

"Ah, I see." So she would be leaving Tallgrass, probably by the end of the year. He had started to care about Alexa, but if he continued, he would be setting himself up to be hurt again. How could he do that to himself or Jana? "When will you know about the scholarship?"

"At the beginning of March I'll find out if I'm a finalist, then the person will be selected by the first of April."

Six weeks. He could keep his distance from her that long. He released her hands and sidled a few feet away, as though that was his first step in severing any emotional ties that had developed since he had gotten to know her.

"I don't hear the music anymore. Maybe that means no more square dancing." Ian moved toward the entrance into the barn.

Her laugh sprinkling the air, Alexa fell into place next to him. "So I guess you aren't gonna sign up for dance lessons?"

"I'll pass."

He entered and looked around until he found his daughter. Jana stood with a group of kids her age. The smile on her face, so like his ex-wife's, caused him to suck in a deep breath. Anger stirred in the pit of his stomach. Jana should have a woman's touch in her life. When Alexa left them at the end of April, what would his daughter do?

What would he do? That question came out of the blue. Did he have more at stake keeping Alexa around than his daughter?

Chapter Nine

After dropping Jana off at home following church on Sunday, Alexa headed to her place. As she turned onto her street, she saw her father's Lincoln Town Car out front. A heaviness sank deep into her heart.

She climbed from her vehicle and spotted her dad sitting on the top step and trudged toward a meeting she couldn't put off any longer. "Mom's gone to lunch with some ladies at the church. She won't be home for a couple of hours." *Why didn't I go with Mom?* Beads of sweat coated her face.

Lord, I don't want to do this. What good will come from talking to him?

"I know. I called her and she told me."

Her rising panic contracted a band around her chest, making each breath difficult. "Then why are you here?"

"To talk to you. This past week talking with your mother has made me rethink a lot about the past."

His grave tone, coupled with his pensive expression, tightened the constriction. Alexa inhaled, and yet it wasn't enough to alleviate the sensation she couldn't get enough oxygen. She couldn't answer him. Instead, she nodded and mounted the stairs to the front door. He followed her into the house.

Alexa tossed her purse on the coffee table and sank into a chair. Several deeper breaths and she finally asked, "What do you want to talk about?"

Her father stood for a few more seconds then selected a place on the couch across from Alexa to sit. "Us. What happened five years ago?"

She shifted, crossing her ankles one direction then the other. Finally she felt compelled to say, "It's the past. Done. Over."

"Is it?" His gaze slid away from hers. "I was—wrong in what I said right before you left home."

Did she hear him right? Folding her hands in her lap, she leaned forward, but she couldn't think of anything to say to his statement.

"Your mother in her not-so-subtle way has been telling me all the things I need to make amends for if I want our marriage to work."

Anger pushed through her shock at his confession that he'd actually done something wrong. "Oh, I see. You're only here because Mom has forced you." She rose. "I have an application to complete and not a lot of time. Thanks for coming by, but you don't need to worry about me. I'm fine." With her hands balled at her sides, she started for the kitchen where she had her paperwork spread out on the table.

"I've hurt you again. I'm not very good at this."

She halted and pivoted. "At what? Making me feel as though I come in second in your life? You've always been very good at that."

"Please take a seat and listen to what I have to say."

The beseeching look on his face nearly undid Alexa. Her

anger deflated, but she remained standing, only a few feet from the kitchen door.

"I wanted you to do what I wanted, but I'm finally realizing I should have listened to you about what *you* wanted. Your mother said she told you about my first wife, Irene, and my son who died in a car wreck. After that I swore I would never love anyone that much. I held my little boy in my arms as he died. With his death, I thought my dreams had died, too."

Her knees went weak. Trembling, Alexa covered the distance to the nearest chair and sank onto it. The love she heard in her father's voice ripped her heart in two. She'd never heard that from him. Part of her wanted to cry at his loss; part of her wanted to wail at her loss—at the opportunity she and her father had never had.

"When I met your mother, I thought I could have the family I always wanted, but not have to give myself totally to the relationship. I've skated along for the past twenty-five years in my marriage on my terms. Your mother has informed me if I want to remain married, that will have to stop. When she left me five weeks ago, I thought she'd come back. Then she didn't. At first I was mad and dealt with her leaving in my usual way—silence." He dropped his gaze to the coffee table, swallowing over and over. "My silence pushed you totally away, and it was going to do the same to your mother." He fixed his attention back on her. "I'm not good at expressing my feelings. Never was, even with Irene, but with her death everything I learned from her died, too."

A lump lodged in Alexa's throat. She put her hands on the arms of the chair and shoved herself to her feet, then closed the distance between her father and her. She hovered in front of him, not sure what to do or say as his pain poured off him and encased her.

"I never told you I loved you, but I do. My bad attempt at showing you my love was trying to control your life, to show you I cared what you did and only wanted the best for you."

"It was your best, not mine." Alexa sat on the coffee table in front of her dad. "As I got older, I wanted some say in my life, but you never would listen. It was your way or no way."

He hung his head. "I know. I still think you'd have made a great doctor. You have such compassion." He looked up at her. "Obviously you got it from your mother, not me."

"But I didn't want to help people that way."

"All I could see was completing the dream I had when my son was born. I wanted him to go into practice with me. We'd heal the world together. Have a practice like none other. I couldn't let go of my past, and it has nearly destroyed my future. I'm going to work to win your mother back, and if you'll give me a chance, you, too. I love you, Alexa."

Tears leaked out of her eyes. She'd waited all her life to hear her father say that. Could she forgive him the twenty-three years of heartache at not hearing the words?

And be ye kind one to another, tenderhearted, forgiving one another, even as God for Christ's sake hath forgiven you. The verse from Ephesians swamped her with feelings she had suppressed for five years—how much she'd wanted her father's love.

"Can you forgive me for what I did?" Her father grasped her hands.

She nodded. Tears knotted her throat and streamed down her face. She fell into his arms and hugged her father—really hugged him for the first time. The feelings of love and awe deluged her with a peace she hadn't experienced as her anger had grown over the years.

"I have too much pride. I let it get in the way of our relationship," her father whispered.

She leaned back. "What are you and Mom gonna do?"

"I don't know. We've talked. She wants to work. I guess I just thought I could provide everything for my family." He gave her a rueful smile. "And I'm discovering I haven't provided anything, really. It has been hard for me to accept. Yesterday she told me she'd only come back if she and I went to a marriage counselor." Shaking his head, he pushed to his feet. "I don't know if I can air my dirty laundry to a stranger. I'm going back home. I've been here longer than I'd planned and I have patients to deal with. And I've got some thinking to do."

She understood where her mother was coming from because in a lot of ways she'd been in the same situation with her father. She'd had to leave to begin discovering who she really was. Pressing her lips together to keep her opinion to herself, she rose and faced her father. "When are you leaving?"

"Right now. If I drive into the night, I can get back to see my patients tomorrow." He came to her, his arms straight at his sides. "I didn't want to leave until I'd at least tried one more time with you. You've been hard to pin down lately."

"I've been avoiding you."

He grinned. "I know." He took her in his embrace and gave her one final hug before parting. "Will you walk me to my car?"

Not a command, a request. "Yes."

Outside on the porch he settled his arm around her shoulders and descended the steps. "I'll call you two and let you know I got home all right. But not until tomorrow morning. No sense waking you up in the middle of the night."

"Always the practical one."

At his vehicle he opened his door then shifted toward

her. His gaze snagged on something behind her for a few seconds then returned to her face. "I think that car is on its last leg. You should look into getting a more reliable one. I can help you if you want. Get something new." He delved into his coat pocket, pulling out his checkbook. "I can give you a down—"

She put her fingers over his mouth. "No. When I get a new used car, it will be because I can pay for it. I appreciate the thought, but this is something I have to do for myself."

"I'm doing it again, aren't I?"

"What? Trying to tell me what to do?"

"Yes."

"I figure you won't change overnight. And besides, finding out your concern comes from love makes all the difference in the world to me."

He kissed her on the cheek and slipped behind the steering wheel. "Hopefully time will break me of that habit."

As Alexa watched her father drive away, she didn't know if he would ever completely change, but for the first time she felt optimism in their relationship.

"They're gonna be here soon. What if my friends don't have fun? Don't want to come over again?" Jana stood in the middle of the den, her teeth digging into her bottom lip.

The past week Jana had been a bundle of nerves as they all had prepared for her birthday party and sleepover. She'd helped Alexa fix the food for the dinner, had gone with her to pick out the cake being served and had helped select the movies to watch.

Alexa started to reply, but Ian walked into the room from the kitchen and made his way toward his daughter. He clasped her shoulders. "It's going to be fine, pumpkin.

Alexa and I will be here if you need us, but only if you need something. Otherwise, you'll have the run of the house."

Her eyes large, Jana pivoted toward Alexa. "But aren't you helping me with the manicures and pedicures?"

"Yes. I wouldn't miss it. We can do them after dinner, but before the movie marathon."

The doorbell chimed.

"I'll get it." Jana raced toward the foyer with Sugar on her heel.

Ian stared at Alexa, moving closer to her. "I feel like I'm getting my daughter back. Lately she's been excited about getting up in the morning, doing activities, going riding at the ranch. Ever since you came into our lives. Are you sure you aren't Mary Poppins in disguise?"

Alexa laughed. "Hardly."

The sound of the bell announced another arrival. Before long, six girls occupied the den, all chatting at once. Ian grabbed Alexa's hand and tugged her toward the kitchen.

"My head is already swelling with all that racket." Ian tapped his temple as if that would shake loose all the chattering that filled it. "Did you do this when you were a child?"

"Only once. My dad didn't like having more than one sleepover. I think it did him in."

"Have you talked with your father this week?"

"He calls every night and talks to both Mom and me. He's wearing her down. But he hasn't quite yet agreed to counseling. I think he feels it's a reflection on him that he can't solve his own problems. He's never been one to accept help easily."

"It can be hard to admit you're wrong." Ian leaned his hip against the counter. "At least you two are really talking."

"Yes, and it feels right. He's actually behind me concerning the scholarship and hopes I get it. He thinks some time abroad will be good for me."

Ian's eyes darkened. "We'd better get the food out for dinner. I do know if the others are like my daughter they'll be ravenous as soon as they stop talking long enough to hear their hungry stomachs growling."

His expression closed down—not one emotion on his face as he turned away from her and headed for the refrigerator to get out the fixings for the tacos. She wasn't sure what to say. Ever since the Valentine's Day party at the ranch, he'd withdrawn some from her. Not that they were dating or had any kind of relationship between them other than employer/employee, but she still hated the wall he'd erected as though it were important to him to keep her at a distance. She missed their talks and camaraderie these past couple of weeks.

She took the meat Jana and she had cooked beforehand and put the glass bowl in the microwave. "My mother won't say anything to my father, but she's lonely. She's gone all the time either working or doing something with a new friend, but I can see it in her eyes when she's home. It won't surprise me if any day I find her packing her bags and returning home."

"How would you feel about that?"

"Glad to get my house back. Sad to see her go. Hopeful that my parents might be able to work things out. In other words, mixed feelings. It's been great getting to know her now that I'm an adult, but she doesn't belong here with me. She just hasn't figured that out yet, or maybe she has and is waiting on my dad. Marriage can be so difficult."

Ian set the shredded cheese on the counter next to the diced tomatoes. "I can attest to that." He glanced toward the den, but the noise coming from that other room hadn't decreased. "I thought my marriage was fine, and I was totally wrong. Yes, we had problems, but what marriage doesn't? But to find your wife gone one day and worse, have her run off with another man, makes a person take a good hard look at his perceptions."

The beep on the microwave echoed through the room. Alexa removed the bowl and set it on the counter with the other ingredients for tacos. "If a marriage is broken, both have to be willing to fix it, not just one. It'll never work. My mother's situation has taught me that, if nothing else. If my father doesn't agree to work with a counselor, I'll have a permanent roommate."

"Dad, is dinner ready? We're hungry," Jana shouted from the den.

Alexa chuckled. "I guess they stopped talking long enough to hear their stomachs rumbling."

Ian walked to the entrance into the den. "Dinner is served."

He couldn't step out of the way fast enough. A flood of girls poured into the room with Ian stuck in the middle of the onslaught. For a second, panic made his eyes saucer round. His gaze swept from one child to the next.

For a short time Alexa had glimpsed the Ian she had been getting to know before the Valentine's Day party. Although the subject matter had been serious, there had been a connection between them, a relaxation of barriers. She wanted that back and wasn't sure how to get it.

"If I had to listen to one more movie about high school girls, cheerleading and puppy love, my eyes were going to cross and my brain was going to shut down." Ian plopped onto the couch in his office and propped his feet up on the coffee table in front of it. "Thanks for suggesting we escape here."

Alexa's mouth dropped open. She'd never seen Ian put his feet clad in shoes up on the furniture like that. "You must be sick." She moved to him and laid her palm against his forehead. "Mmm. Normal. Are you one of those people whose standard temperature is below 98.6 degrees?"

"Cute. Why do you think I'm sick?"

She pointed to his casual pose then flicked the tips of his tennis shoes. "Not only are your feet up, but you hardly ever wear tennis shoes, except when you jog. Most of the time you wear a pair of loafers."

"I didn't realize you kept track of my attire." A sparkle in his eyes accentuated his amusement.

Heat scored her cheeks. She stepped away, desperately wanting to fan herself but refraining. Whatever possessed her to touch him like that and admit she paid attention to what he wore? She didn't want him to get the wrong idea. "I'm very observant. A teacher has to be. It's part of the training we receive." If any more excuses tumbled out, she would die of embarrassment. She spun around and searched for something to take his mind off her keen observation skills when it came to him. "I see you have a chess set."

"Do you play?"

"Well, no. But I play checkers."

He laughed. "Not quite the same thing." After putting his feet back on the floor, he rose. "But wait here. I'll be right back."

Two minutes later he reentered his office with a checkers set. "Let's play. I had to go through the gauntlet of questions to get this, so we're going to use it."

"Yes, sir." She flashed him a smile.

Ian pulled up a chair across from the couch with the coffee table between them, then he set the checkerboard up. "Red or black?"

"I love bright colors, so red."

A cheer came from the direction of the den. "I think the

boy finally got the gal. Do they not see it's the same plot as all the other teen movies?"

"Ah, but it's love. And girls are in love with the idea of finding Mr. Right."

"At eleven and twelve?"

"Probably before that. I had a crush on a guy in third grade, and he wouldn't give me the time of day on the playground." She made her first move on the board.

Ian plowed his hand through his hair, managing to mess it up. "This is gonna be a l*ooo*ng night."

"Yep." Alexa checked her watch. "But I've got to leave in an hour, or I'll turn into a pumpkin."

"Wasn't that the coach in the fairy tale, not Cinderella? Or was that Snow White? Or Sleeping Beauty? I get those fairy tales mixed up." On his third turn, he jumped her red piece.

She countered by hopping over two of his black ones. "It was Cinderella, and I guess I should say I'd turn into a raggedly dressed servant girl, limping home with only one shoe on. Which, with my car, could happen."

"When you get home, call me to let me know you arrived safely. You really do need a more reliable car."

"You sound like my father."

"That would be something a father says to his daughter. We only want our children to be safe."

"Yeah, I know, and when he told me that right before he left to go back home, I didn't get upset."

Ian glanced up from the board and pinned her with an intense look that held her entranced until he grinned, peered down and made a move, jumping her red pieces three times then saying, "King me."

The rest of the game went quickly with Ian winning. Alexa couldn't keep her mind focused on any kind of strategy to counter him. All her thoughts revolved around the man across from her, his tousled hair, his long sleeves rolled up on his button-down shirt, the worn-looking jeans with tennis shoes peeking out of the bottom. Casual. Relaxed, with a smile deep in his warm blue eyes. Totally riveted on her at the moment.

Her heartbeat accelerated. She drew in a deep breath, than another one. He reached across the expanse and clasped her hands. As he rose, he tugged her up, too. His gaze still trained on her, he skirted the coffee table and drew her against him.

"So little time before you have to leave. I've tried to keep my distance." He combed strands of her hair from her face, murmuring, "But it's not working," then framed it with his large hands, his palm prints like a mark, searing his claim. "I'm beginning to feel like Prince Charming at the ball."

He bent toward her and brushed his mouth across hers once then twice, tentative explorations, before his arms encased her in a tight embrace and his mouth declared his intentions. His lips, like his palms, branded her his in that moment. His assertion blasted through all her defenses and seized her heart. She was his.

"Dad," Jana called from the hallway, "it's midnight and we want you to tell us that great scary story you know."

Jana's voice floated to Alexa, nipping at her consciousness. She needed to do something. But what? Then suddenly the fact that she was hugging Ian, his mouth whispering kisses across her cheek, flooded her. She quickly stepped back as his daughter appeared in the doorway. Alexa swept around to mask her flaming-hot cheeks.

She pressed her hands to her face while she heard Ian say, "I'll be there in a sec."

"What have you two been doing?"

Alexa fortified herself with a deep breath and turned

slowly, praying she'd managed to school a calm expression on her face. "Checkers." The little squeak at the end was a dead giveaway something else had happened besides the game.

"Oh. Dad's great at that game. I should have warned you, Alexa. Will you stay for the scary story? We're gonna turn the lights off and everything."

"I'd better pass." She made a production out of checking her new watch. "Mom will worry. I told her I'd be home a little after twelve." *And if I don't leave soon, I'll want another kiss. And another.*

Jana crossed the room to Alexa and hugged her. "Thanks for making my birthday so special. I'll see you tomorrow morning for breakfast."

"I'll be here. I love making pancakes with all the fixings." The feel of the child's arms around her where her father's had been moments before underscored how important this family had become to her. The thought, along with the effect Ian's kiss had on her, terrified her. She didn't want to care and lose them.

After Jana left the office, Alexa started for the door without looking at Ian. She didn't know what to feel, but she was falling for a man who was still struggling with his past, who hadn't made his peace with God. She needed to get her life back on track and let him work through his past. He'd never be able to really move on until he did. And she wouldn't settle for second best. Her father had at least taught her that.

"You're so good for my daughter," Ian murmured, but instead of a smile, his eyebrows scrunched together as though that statement had forced him to face something he didn't like.

Alexa hurried toward the hallway and opened the coat closet near the foyer. After grabbing her jacket and purse, she crossed the entryway, aware Ian's gaze was on her. At the front door she glanced back.

He strode to her. "Don't forget to call and let me know you made it home okay."

With her heart swelling into her throat and making any words difficult, she nodded and left. Ian stood on the porch and watched her until she pulled out of the driveway. Fifteen minutes later she parked at her duplex, all her doubts about Ian and her ever having any kind of relationship nibbling at her composure.

Before she let herself into her house, she took her cell phone out and placed a call to Ian. "I arrived safe and sound. How's it going? Did you manage to scare the girls?"

"They ran from the den screaming."

Noise, some screams, filtered through the connection. "Really?"

He chuckled. "No. They thought I did a lousy job and booted me from the room. Now they're taking turns scaring each other."

"It's sounding like they'll doing a great job."

"That's Jana. I'm in the kitchen listening, and I'm getting scared. She's got quite an imagination."

"Yeah, that's your daughter."

"You've brought that out in her. You know that's one of your talents, bringing out the best in people."

His voice, a deep baritone, washed over her like a heavy fog rolling in. Alexa sank back against the door, the energy siphoning from her legs. "Thanks."

"Good night, Alexa. I'll see you in less than seven hours."

Seven hours when she didn't think she was going to sleep a wink. She clicked off her cell and stuffed it back into her purse. She started to turn to unlock the front door, when it opened and she nearly fell through the entrance.

Her mother steadied Alexa then shut the door and locked it. "I saw you pull up. I was getting worried when you didn't come in."

"Ian just wanted me to let him know I made it home all right." Alexa stooped down to greet Charlie and rubbed him behind the ears.

"How was the birthday party?"

"Jana's having a great time." Alexa set her bag on the table in the small foyer. "Why are you up so late?"

"Because I wanted to tell you that I'm going to Tulsa early tomorrow to pick up your father. He's flying in. I'm going home with him, and he'll drive my car." Her mom headed into the living room. "He told me tonight he's set up our first counseling session next Thursday."

"Great. I'm thrilled you two are gonna work things out."

Her mother faced her. "You and your dad have really mended your fences?"

"We're working on it." Alexa turned to leave. "I need to get some sleep. Good—"

"A registered letter came for you today. I signed for it. It's from the foundation you applied to for the scholarship. I started to call you, but I didn't want to mess up Jana's birthday. I even thought about opening it to see if you're a finalist. I can't wait any longer." Her mom snatched an envelope from the coffee table and thrust it into Alexa's hands.

She stared at her typed address, her hands beginning to tremble.

"What are you waiting for?"

Alexa tore into the envelope and unfolded the letter. The word *congratulations* jumped off the paper. "'Congratulations. You are one of four finalists for the Christian Teachers International Scholarship. The competition was tough this year, but your application stood out from a total of over five hundred.'"

Her mother hugged her. "You're a shoo-in. I know it."

But all Alexa could think about was how this would affect her relationship with Ian and Jana.

Chapter Ten

The next morning after all the girls filled their plates with buttermilk pancakes and fruit and settled in the den, Alexa sank into a chair across from Ian at the kitchen table with her own plate. She poured maple syrup over her pancakes.

"These are delicious," Ian said after taking a bite of his breakfast.

"It's my grandma's recipe. I have to admit I'm hungry."

He glanced toward the den. "It's awfully quiet in there. That's different. They were talking all night long. I didn't know kids had that much to talk about."

"They wind down after a while. I imagine they're exhausted. Talking takes a lot of energy."

"I'm beginning to believe listening does, too. I lost count of how many boys they discussed. My daughter went on and on about Randy. Did you know he has dreamy eyes according to Jana?" His mouth hitched up at one corner. "I can't emphasize enough I'm not ready for my daughter to be interested in boys."

"I don't think it matters if you are or not. She is."

"Has she ever talked to you about—boys?"

His hesitation at the word *boys* sparked a chuckle from Alexa. "She's asked me what I think about Randy."

"And?" Ian forked another bite of pancakes into his mouth.

"I think he's a nice kid. He's polite, interacts with the others when he's here for your class. He and Jana had fun together at the Valentine's Day party."

Washing his food down with a swallow of coffee, Ian gave her a thoughtful look. "Mmm. Maybe Randy ought to graduate to the next level of math."

"It won't stop them from talking. He's often out at the ranch riding. And she told me he was at the HHH meeting she went to with you."

"I guess I should be thankful for him. It's motivated her to go to the weekly meetings and to the ranch. Him and Ashley." His gaze locked with hers. "And you."

The intensity in his eyes brought back all the feelings his kiss had created last night. She wanted to experience that again, and yet she knew the danger in it. Each day she was with him she surrendered another piece of her heart to him.

"This is when Jana needs a woman's touch. I'm concerned when she gets older she's going to have questions for me I can't answer," Ian continued.

"Probably, but you'll do the best you can."

"Does she ever talk about her mother?" Ian took another sip of his coffee.

"A couple of times. She wonders where she is. I think the therapist she's been seeing is helping her a lot concerning her mother."

"She hasn't said anything about the fact she hasn't received a present from her yet?"

"Yeah, but her birthday isn't technically until Monday. I think she expects something that day."

"What if Tracy doesn't send anything this time? She did

last year and at Christmas, but I can't control if she does or doesn't."

"And that aggravates you."

"Not being able to control it?"

"Yes."

Ian shoved his chair back and pushed to his feet. "This is my daughter we're talking about. Wouldn't it bother you?"

His question, although spoken quietly, held intensity in it that conveyed his conflicting emotions—frustration, anger and perhaps even love—concerning his wife. "Yes. All I can say is be here for her if that happens." Did he still love her? Was this what it was really about? Tracy had left him, not the other way around. Ian kissing her might not mean much to him, not like it did to her.

"I've even thought about buying something and wrapping it and pretending it was from Tracy."

"You can't protect Jana forever."

Ian snatched up his mug and strode to the stove to refill his coffee. With a glance toward the den, he said, "I know." When he sat back in his chair and leaned close to Alexa, he added, "But she's doing so well lately. I'd hate to see her backslide because of Tracy."

Was Ian talking just about Jana or also himself? Alexa studied his suddenly neutral expression and couldn't tell. "Talking about mothers, mine is returning home with my father in the next few days. She's gone to Tulsa to pick him up at the airport."

"That's good news."

"Yeah, and I'm looking forward to seeing my dad again. I'm liking that feeling."

"So you've totally forgiven him?"

"Yes, once I made up my mind to. Each day it gets easier and easier."

Alexa dropped her gaze to her mug of tea. She needed to tell Ian about the scholarship. He'd wanted to know when she heard, and yet she hated to end the conversation. Every time she'd brought up the subject before with Ian, the atmosphere had chilled afterward. She wanted to do what she and Daniel had planned to do five years ago. This scholarship would allow her to and pay off her student loans. On the other hand, her feelings about Ian were growing every time she was around him, and being away from him would doom any relationship that was developing between them. As much as she wished differently, she didn't think their timing was good. He wasn't in the same place as she was.

"When I went home last night, I got some other news besides my mother and father's getting back together." She paused and inhaled a soothing breath while Ian lifted his mug toward his mouth. "I was notified I am one of the four finalists for the scholarship I applied for last month."

His drink halted in midair. He stared at her. For a few seconds his jaw set in a firm line, then as though he shook himself, his expression eased into a bland one. His hand completed its trek, and he sipped his coffee. "They would have been foolish if they hadn't pick you. Congratulations."

She blushed, the warmth fanning out from her cheeks to cover her face. "Thank you, but it doesn't mean I'll get the scholarship. There are three others competing for it."

"What happens next?"

"I go for an interview in Oklahoma City in two weeks on a Friday. I'll need to take the day off."

"I've got a better suggestion. Jana and I will go with you. We'll make it an outing. When you aren't interviewing, we can go to the zoo or the Science Museum of Oklahoma right next door to the zoo. Both places are great educational tools for Jana."

"You're just afraid my car won't make it," Alexa said with a laugh.

"True. I don't trust your car outside the city limits of Tallgrass." He rapped the side of his chin. "Come to think of it, I don't trust your car at all. I've known you two months and it has broken down three times that I know of. Not what I call reliable."

"I know. I keep hearing that from you and Dad. But it takes money to get a new one. It will have to do for now." She rose and gathered up their empty plates. "But since I want to make my interview, I'm gonna take you up on your offer, and in exchange I'll come over on the following Saturday and entertain your daughter while you work to make up the time you'll miss on that Friday. Deal?"

"Deal."

Barking erupted from the den. Both Ian and Alexa turned toward the sound, then looked at each other.

"Sugar's begging again." Alexa placed the dirty dishes in the sink and started for the room.

"You mean my daughter isn't feeding her fast enough. If she eats too much extra food, I'll have to take her jogging with me."

"Exercise is good for dogs." Alexa stopped in the entrance and zoomed in on Jana and Ashley slipping Sugar some bacon. "Did everyone get enough?"

The girls swiveled their attention to Alexa. Several piped in saying yes while Jana and Ashley said no.

"Maybe if you would stop feeding Sugar so much, you'd have some for yourselves." Ian stepped around Alexa and covered the distance to the dog, sitting practically on top of his daughter's plate of half-eaten pancakes.

"That's okay, Dad. I'll just finish off the chips and dip we didn't eat last night."

"Not for breakfast." Ian scooped up Jana's pet. Sugar began wiggling, wanting down. "Parents will be here in half an hour. Time to clean up."

A few groans accompanied that suggestion. Alexa turned back into the kitchen and went to the sink to do her own cleaning up. While filling the dishwasher, she thought about the trip in two weeks to Oklahoma City with Ian and Jana. Like a family. That thought threw her off balance. The plate in her hand nearly slipped from her fingers. Quickly she tightened her grip, but the idea of being a family with Ian and Jana wouldn't leave her mind.

Monday afternoon Alexa returned to Ian's after having lunch with her parents. The meal had been at a little café, and she'd enjoyed herself. For the first time she really felt free of the burden from her past. The Lord knew what He was doing when He said to forgive others.

Ian pulled the door open, and the smile that Alexa had on her face disappeared. Worry wrinkled his forehead.

"What's wrong?" Alexa entered the house.

"The mail came and no present from Tracy for Jana. I tried talking to her, but she took Sugar and is out back on the bench. She told me she didn't want to talk about it when I went out there fifteen minutes ago to take her a sweater." He combed his fingers through his hair. "Will you see if she'll talk to you? Maybe a woman's touch will help."

"Of course." Alexa made her way out back. She knew a little of what Jana was going through because so much of her life she hadn't thought her father loved her. *Please, Lord, help me to connect with Jana.*

When Alexa slipped onto the bench next to the child, hugging Sugar to her chest, Jana glanced at Alexa. "Did Dad send ya out here?"

"I came because I thought you might want to talk."

"I don't want to talk about Mom."

"Then let's talk about something else. Did your dad tell you about the trip to Oklahoma City at the end of next week?"

"Yeah, at lunch. You have some kind of interview with some people for a scholarship."

"If I get the scholarship, I'll get to become a teacher faster and graduate in December."

"You're a teacher already. You're mine."

Alexa smiled at Jana. "Thanks. I love teaching you, but I'm only here until tax season is over with." She needed to remind Jana, but also herself. Her job would soon end, and she would no longer see them as much. A heaviness in her heart emphasized how much she had come to care for both Jana and Ian. Who was she kidding? It was more than caring. And again she knew her heart would be broken, as when Daniel died.

"But I don't want ya to leave."

"We'll still see each other. Do you think when I stop working here I won't see you anymore?"

Jana nodded then buried her face against Sugar.

"No way. You can't get rid of me that easily. When I care about someone, they're part of my life *always*."

"Does that mean my mom doesn't care about me?" The child kept her head down.

The question hovered in the air between them. The tightness in Alexa's chest swelled, threatening her next breath. "I can't answer for your mom. I can answer for me. You're such a special young lady. I'll always care about you. And when I'm no longer your teacher, I hope we'll still be friends even if we are apart sometimes."

Jana lifted her tear-streaked face. "I can come visit ya at your house?"

"Anytime, and you can call when you need to talk. My feelings for you won't change. In fact, if anything, they'll grow the more we get to know each other."

"Then what's wrong with me that my mother doesn't want to see me or talk to me?"

Nothing, baby. It's your mom's problem. But Alexa refrained from saying that and instead said, "I never told you about my relationship with my father while I was growing up. I thought for years he didn't love me because his way of showing love was by telling me what I needed to do. He thought he was showing his love because he cared enough to try to get me to do what he thought was best. All I thought was he didn't love me. He never hugged me or told me he did. I needed the words. He didn't know how to express them. Some people are like that. It doesn't mean they don't feel it. They may, in fact, think they are showing it to their loved one. But I know now he does love me. I may not hear the words often, but he still feels that way."

"So ya think my mom loves me?"

"Frankly, I can't see her not loving you. You're one of a kind. Unique." Alexa peered at the house and spied Ian standing in the bay window in the den. "And you have a father who loves you so much. He's concerned about you."

"I know." Jana scrubbed the tears from her cheeks. "I need to let him know I'm okay."

"Are you okay?"

"Yeah. I just thought of a girl in my Sunday-school class who doesn't even have a mother alive. She told me her dad is too busy working, and she stays at her grandmother's a lot. My dad moved his business to our house for me. He gives me his time even when I know he's extra busy right now."

"Then let's go let your dad know you're all right."

Jana rose, putting Sugar on the ground. "I've been teaching her to stay near me so we don't always have to use a leash when we go outside."

"So no more encounters with the geese?"

"Nope." Jana started for the house. "Dad told me we're going to the zoo and museum after your interview."

"It's a school day, so you're gonna do some schoolwork while we're there, and when you get back, I'll want you to write me a story about your trip. What you liked. What you didn't like."

Jana giggled. "You're such a hard teacher."

"I've gotta earn my paycheck."

Ian opened the back door, one eyebrow raised as Jana and Alexa went inside.

"I understand there's some double-chocolate birthday cake still left over. I don't know about you two, but I could use some chocolate today." Alexa mouthed the word *okay* to Ian when Jana turned away.

Nodding, he grinned. "Ah, a woman after my own heart."

His teasing words sank into Alexa's heart, endearing him to her even more. "I'll get it."

"Speaking of eating, Dad and I are going out tonight to dinner at the inn near the highway."

Alexa lifted the lid to reveal a half-eaten triple-layer chocolate cake and brought it to the table. On her return trip to get the plates and forks, she said, "I hear the food is delicious."

"You want to come with us?" Jana plopped down in her chair and scooped some rich frosting onto her fingertip then licked it off.

Without looking at Ian, Alexa retrieved the knife and other items and started back to the table. "No, I have a term paper I need to finish tonight, and besides, this is a special date between father and daughter."

"But you're part of the fam—" The rest of the child's words faded as she looked down at her lap. "You should come. Don't ya think, Dad?" Jana lifted pleading eyes to her father.

"Alexa is welcome to come, but if it's her decision not to, we need to honor it."

"Dad? Alexa? This is *my* birthday." Jana shifted her attention between Alexa and her father.

Alexa opened her mouth to change her answer, but the doorbell rang. Ian rose and hurried across the kitchen to answer it.

Jana leaned toward Alexa. "Please come."

"You don't want to go by yourself with your father?"

"I have dinner by myself with him all the time." Jana averted her gaze as though she was hiding something.

"Jana, what's going on?"

"Nothing," the young girl answered way too fast and high-pitched.

"Hon, you've got a package from your mother." Ian strode toward the table and set the gift in front of his daughter.

The child's eyes grew big as she tore into the present. Inside was a beautiful denim dress with sparkles and sequins. Jana opened the card from her mother and read, "'I had fun shopping for you. Kisses and hugs, Mom.'"

No "I love you." Alexa shifted her attention to Ian, whose expression darkened, his eyebrows slashing down. But the second his daughter peered toward him, his angry look dissolved into a neutral one.

Slowly the corners of his mouth lifted. "You see, pumpkin? She didn't forget your birthday. You should wear that dress tonight."

Jana flew out of her chair and into her father's arms. "I love you, Daddy. Talk Alexa into coming to eat with us."

Ian swung his beseeching gaze toward Alexa. "Please. We'll only be gone a few hours, and you can leave early today so you can work on your paper."

Alexa laughed. "You two are quite a team. Okay. But you have to get me home by nine. No later." She refused to think too much on the hours she would have to stay up in order to go with Ian and Jana, but she wouldn't change her mind this time. "If you're gonna dress up, Jana, then I'm gonna have to, too."

"I liked what you wore to church yesterday."

"What?" Ian sat at the table.

"It's a secret." Alexa winked at Jana. "It'll be a surprise tonight."

"Yeah, Dad. If you came to church with us, you'd know."

"I just might have to. I don't like surprises."

That evening after having a nice dinner at the inn, Ian pulled into Alexa's driveway. He glanced back in his rearview mirror and noticed that Jana had curled up on the seat and fallen asleep.

"I'm not surprised she's finally slowed down long enough to fall asleep. Ever since her birthday party Friday night, she has been going strong. Staying up late, getting up early. Girlfriends calling all the time. Jana talking to them for hours." He opened the car door, and light flooded the interior. "I'm going to have to consider getting my daughter a cell phone."

"Girls do like to chat."

Ian slid his gaze over Alexa, wearing an ankle-length dress with large yellow flowers with touches of green and white. It suited her and looked good on her, soft and feminine. Two months ago he would have been surprised by the fact her brightly colored attire appealed to him, but not anymore.

"Tell me about it. I could hardly get a word in edgewise tonight at the restaurant," he finally said, realizing he'd been staring at her and she knew it.

Her head tilted at an angle, she looked at him up through her eyelashes. "Sorry about that. Thanks for a lovely evening."

"You're welcome." A link sprang up between them that caught Ian in a snare.

He was falling for Alexa, and he shouldn't. What if she won the scholarship and had to leave for three years after she graduated in December? Although it wasn't the same as what Tracy had done, he didn't want someone important in Jana's life to be yanked away again. She was too fragile. It was best if he backed off now—before Jana became too used to Alexa being a part of their lives. Before he became too used to it, as well.

"I'll walk you to your door." His words sounded forced to his ears, but he couldn't shake the thought of what he was going to do when Alexa was no longer in *his* life, not just Jana's. He climbed out and rounded the front of his vehicle.

Before he had a chance to open the car door for her, she did and had even started for her house. "It's not like this is a date or anything. You don't have to walk me to my porch."

It had felt like a date, even with Jana accompanying them. "No, but I want to." He slipped his arm around her shoulders so naturally the action surprised him for a second, but when he thought about it, it felt right.

Standing in front of her door, she faced him. "I hope you'll go with Jana and me to church this Sunday. I think it's only a matter of time before she starts going to the youth group for her age."

"Great. Anytime she attends functions outside of home and especially without me shows she's healing." *Now if only I can.* Today when he'd watched his daughter pull into herself because she hadn't heard from Tracy, his anger festered anew in the pit of his stomach. How could Jana's mother do that to her? And the fact that a gift had arrived later still hadn't appeased that anger.

"I certainly think she's making progress. She goes to the store with me, the ranch and church, all without you now."

"I'm going to have to tag along to the ranch again. I enjoyed our ride. It brings back some fond memories as a child growing up in Texas. My best friend lived on a ranch, and I rode all the time with him." He moved close, at first planning to open the screen door for Alexa, but instead found himself taking her hands in his and lifted them up between their bodies.

He stared into her warm chocolate-brown eyes and wanted to pull her into his arms. A smile slowly brightened her gaze and a soft sigh escaped her slightly parted lips. Lips he had to kiss.

Leaning toward her, unable to resist her, he grazed his mouth over hers, then released her hands to encircle his arms around her and tug her flat against him. He deepened the kiss until she drove all thoughts of Tracy from his mind. His attention totally focused on the woman in his embrace, her scent of vanilla swirling around him and tempting him to forget any need to keep Alexa at a distance—from touching his heart.

When he parted, he laid his forehead against hers and framed her face in his hands. "I was so wrong about you."

"How so?" Breathlessness accompanied each word.

"I thought you were all wrong for Jana." *And for me.*

"But not now?"

Drawing back, he ran his thumbs across her cheeks. "No."

"Thank you. That means a lot to me." She covered his hands on her face. "I know that day at the restaurant it wasn't easy for you to come and ask me to work for you after turning me down for Attila the Hun."

"Don't remind me of that. Jana was right. I like things to run smoothly, but that woman was worse than a drill sergeant."

"I still have several hours' worth of work to do, so I'd better go in." She rummaged for her house key as Ian opened the screen door. Throwing a glance over her shoulder, she grinned. "Good night."

The urge to pull her into his embrace held him frozen to the spot even after she had gone inside. He opened and closed his hands at his sides. The feel of her lips seared into his memory. Her scent still taunted him. That smell would always remind him of Alexa from now on.

With a shake of his head, he strode toward his car, needing to get control of his feelings before he ended up loving a woman who wasn't going to stay around. It wasn't just Jana he wanted to protect but himself, too. He couldn't go through what Tracy had done to him again. Wasn't that why he told himself he wouldn't fall in love with another woman?

As he slid behind the steering wheel, he heard Jana in the backseat. He angled toward her. "How long have you been up?" *Did you see me kiss Alexa?*

"Not long." She moved to the front seat where Alexa had been moments before. "I had a great time tonight. Did ya?"

"Well, yes. The meal was good."

"And Alexa looked beautiful. I like her hair down like she wore it. Don't you?"

What's his daughter doing? "Yeah, down is nice." *Easier for him to run his hands through it. Whoa, there, Ferguson. Not a good thought for a man who vowed not to fall for another woman.*

By the time he arrived home, Jana had grilled him about

the evening until he wanted to scream. Halfway through the interrogation he knew what his daughter was up to. She was trying to get him and Alexa together. He hoped she hadn't seen the kiss, or she would double her efforts and he'd have a hard time evading her tactics. He just didn't know where she got her persistence.

When he came into his house, he tossed his keys in the basket on the desk in the kitchen and checked the messages on his phone. Two were from clients, and he'd return them tomorrow morning, but the voice of the last one shuddered through him.

"This is Tracy. I wanted to wish Jana a happy birthday. Please have her call me." She proceeded to rattle off her number.

Her whispery voice, so cheerful, as though nothing had happened in the past year and a half, gutted him. He sank onto the chair nearby.

Jana rushed into the kitchen. "Dad, I thought I heard Mom." She scanned the room.

He inhaled a deep breath then another, but nothing relieved the tight band around his chest. "She left a message for you." After punching the button to replay it, he collapsed back against the chair and listened again to the woman who'd betrayed him. All their dealings concerning the divorce had gone through their lawyers. This was the first time he'd heard her since she'd walked away from their marriage and it left him empty, as though he'd been hollowed out. Helplessness swamped him.

"Can I call her?"

Jana's eager question brought him back to the present. He nodded, the past leaving a trail of numbness.

His daughter snatched up the phone and started to punch in the numbers. "I didn't get all of them."

He had. Numbers always stuck in his mind. This one he wished hadn't. His hand quivered as he finished placing the call for Jana.

"Mom!" Jana paused, her expression radiating her excitement. "Yeah, I love the dress you bought me. Thanks! When are you coming home?" Another long pause. "Okay, I hope you will."

As Ian listened to his daughter talk with her mother, bitterness coated his tongue with a metallic taste. Then he realized he'd bit down so hard, he'd cut the inside of his mouth. Just when he was starting to pull his life together, Tracy had to interfere. She didn't have the right to waltz back into their lives.

He'd loved her once. What had he done wrong? Why hadn't his love been enough to hold her here? All his doubts surfaced and filled the hollowness. How in the world did he even briefly think a relationship might work with Alexa?

Chapter Eleven

"**I**'d say this has been a perfect day. The weather is beautiful." Alexa peered up at the cloudless sky in the middle of the Oklahoma City Zoo. "Where to next?"

Jana studied the map in her hand. "We've got to see the kangaroos, and I can't miss the pygmy hippo. Hippos are so cute."

Ian leaned in and whispered into Alexa's ear, "Sort of like Sugar. So ugly they are cute."

"See, I knew Sugar would grow on you." His light musky scent vied with the smells of the various animals and the vegetation.

"I wish I could have brought Sugar." Jana started off in the direction of the kangaroos, turning around and walking backward. "And we need to see the elephants, rhinos, oh, and the gorillas." She whirled around and increased her pace.

"In other words, everything." Ian took off after his daughter.

"It'll be interesting Monday to see what she decides to write about this trip." Hurrying to keep up with the pair, Alexa thought back to the interview she'd had concerning the scholarship earlier that morning. It had gone well, but she wouldn't count on getting the money. It was in the Lord's hands now.

At the kangaroo enclosure Jana watched for a few minutes, compressing her lips in a thoughtful expression. "I'd like to go to Australia one day. Do ya think we could, Dad?"

Ian's eyes widened. "You really want to travel?"

"I want to see the world. There's so much to see."

Ian's mouth hung open. "You do? Since when?"

"Since Alexa and I have been studying the different countries." Jana peered around her father to Alexa. "I want to study Australia next. They have such cute animals."

"Then Australia will be after we finish up Kenya."

"The pygmy hippo exhibition is over there." After pointing to the right, Jana headed toward the area.

Ian shook his head. "Is that my daughter? Up until three months ago she didn't like to leave the house without me."

"She didn't say she wanted to go by herself. I think she wants to see it with you. But I am glad she's interested in what's going on in the world. Her interest started with the animals. First the ones in Brazil, then Africa."

Following his daughter, Ian glanced at Alexa next to him on the path. "I know she talks about what she's learning, but I didn't realize it was to the point she wanted to see some of the places."

"She's here in Oklahoma City. And remember when we were hanging the posters in the classroom and she talked about seeing some of those places?"

"Are you giving her ideas because that's what you want, to see the world?"

Alexa stopped short of Jana near the pygmy hippo enclosure. "I'm not giving her any ideas. I'm opening up her mind to what's out there. She has to make her own decisions about what she learns and retains."

Since his daughter's birthday dinner and the kiss on her porch, he'd withdrawn from her again, burying himself in the office and only coming out for lunch and an occasional pass-through to get something he needed. At first she'd thought it was because April fifteenth was less than a month away and he had a lot of work, but now she wasn't so sure it wasn't something else, too. She suspected it was because Tracy had called Jana the evening of her birthday. Jana had told her the next day, but Ian hadn't said a word about the call. The silence underscored all the reasons they would never work out and that she needed to go ahead with her own plans.

He dropped his head and kneaded his nape. "I know you aren't. I don't know why I said that."

"You don't?" *Tell me about Tracy and the call.*

"I suppose all your talk about the scholarship and what it means. You teaching in some underdeveloped country, helping others. How much you've always wanted to travel and see what's out there. And now my daughter is talking like that."

"And you like the familiarity of Tallgrass?"

"I know what to expect." He gave her a rueful smile. "Well, usually."

Ah, it gives him a sense of control. Hasn't the phone call from Tracy shown him he doesn't really have control? He can control what he does but not what others do. "I wish we could control everything, but we can't whether we live in Tallgrass or the Amazon. Life is a risk. You can't plan it. It has a way of throwing you a curve when you least expect it."

"Hey, you guys. Are you ready to move on?" Jana came

up to them and tugged on her father's hand. "There's so much to see, and we still have the museum to go through."

Two weeks after the excursion to the zoo Alexa reentered the den after showing the man who gave Jana guitar lessons to the door. The tension in the house was palpable. When Ian had let her in this morning, with dark circles under his eyes and mussed hair, as though he hadn't bothered with combing it when he woke up, she'd known something wasn't right. No matter what she did, he held himself apart from her the whole morning and into the afternoon. At lunch for the first time, he'd eaten at his desk in his office.

"Mom called me again last night." Jana put her guitar back into its case after finishing her lesson.

Now she understood what was going on with Ian. "She did? What did she have to say?"

"She's coming to Tallgrass next week. Her and her husband are passing through on their way to Chicago. She's gonna stay a few days and see me."

Alexa studied Jana's expression, usually so open, but at the moment neutral. A dark glint in the child's eyes, however, told Alexa conflicting emotions were battling for dominance in the young girl who had struggled with her mother's abandonment. "How do you feel about that?"

"When I heard from her on my birthday, I was excited at first. I didn't want to do anything to make her not call again. But now I don't know. Why didn't she call me before?"

"Have you asked her?" Alexa had learned the hard way with her own father that keeping her emotions inside didn't make the situation better in the long run.

"No, I'm afraid to. I want to see her. I need to see her. But when I told Dad last night, I could tell he was very upset. I'm sure you can tell that, too. You need to help him."

"Me?" The word squeaked out in surprise.

"Yeah, he likes you. You make him laugh. And I saw him kiss you on my birthday."

So Jana had been watching them on the porch. Had she really been asleep? Little things the child had done over the past month or so led her to believe Jana was trying to fix up Ian and her. The invitation to eat dinner the evening of her birthday was a good example, and she wasn't sure what to do about Ian, because under all that anger he manifested toward Tracy, Alexa couldn't help wondering if he was still in love with his ex-wife.

"Do you know he's cleaned up his work area in the garage? I saw him last week late at night. I couldn't sleep and got up to get something to eat. I saw him picking up several of his tools. He even brought out something he hadn't finished and placed it on his work bench."

"I didn't have anything to do with that."

"Yes, you did."

The thought that she could have helped Ian made her heart sing, then she remembered how he had been acting the past few weeks—withdrawn, deep in his own thoughts. It was more than his heavy workload. "Jana, you're reading something into a situation that isn't there."

"I don't want you to leave at the end of the month. You understand me. You care about me. Mom's gonna come here for a few days and move on. I…" Jana swallowed the rest of her words, her eyes misting.

Alexa folded her arms around Jana, her growing feelings for the child—and her father—thickening her throat with her own tears. "Just because I won't be here every day as your tutor doesn't mean I won't see you. You can't get rid of me that easily. I'm in your life now as a friend." She pulled back, cupping the girl's chin and lifting it. "I take being friends very seriously. And my feelings aren't gonna change concerning you."

"Mom's did."

"I'm not your mother. When you become my friend, you become my friend for life."

"Is Dad a friend?"

"Yes, of course."

"Then help him."

"I'll try."

The following Thursday, Alexa rapped her knuckles against Ian's closed office door. Her stomach constricted as though riddled with tiny knots.

"Come in."

When she entered the room, she came to a halt a few feet inside and blinked at the chaotic mess surrounding Ian. Stacks of folders—but not in their neat little piles—littered his desk, some even on the floor. The blinds behind him were still drawn, little light leaking through the slats although it was early afternoon and bright and sunny outside.

"Is this what it's like a week before April fifteenth?" She waved her arm about at the clutter.

He scanned his office. "Not usually."

"Then what's happened? I would think someone snatched the real Ian and replaced him with you."

He arched an eyebrow. "More clients."

"Is that really what it is? You're never disorganized and frankly this is, for want of a better word, a mess."

"Maybe you're rubbing off on me."

"Ouch! I may not be organized like you, but I'm not messy."

He heaved a deep sigh. "You're right and I shouldn't

have said that." He typed something on his computer then looked at her again. "What do you need?"

"I'll come back later. This obviously isn't a good time to talk."

"Later won't be either. Not for the next seven days, especially since Tracy has decided to visit Jana tomorrow. I think she purposely picked my busiest time to come back to Tallgrass finally. Now I have to worry about Jana and how she's gonna take this visit, because her mother will leave again."

"You'll be there for her like you've always been."

"But will it be enough?"

"I'm not gonna tell you she won't miss her mother. She will. But you and your love will fill the void."

Dropping his head, he rubbed his fingertips into his brow. "A girl should have a special bond with her mother."

"In a perfect world, yes. A bond between a father and daughter is special, too. Don't forget that."

Ian peered at his computer screen for a long moment. "What did you need to see me about?"

Alexa stuck her hand in her pocket and fingered the letter she'd received from the Christian Teachers International Organization. She needed to tell them if she was going to accept the scholarship by April sixteenth. She didn't want to wait to the last minute to tell Ian and Jana.

Fortifying herself with a deep inhalation, she moved forward and sank into the chair in front of his desk. When his gaze pinned hers down, she wanted to tear it away but couldn't. "Yesterday I received notification that I got the scholarship."

The slight narrowing of his look was the only indication he even heard what she'd said. Then his mouth tightened, and he looked back at the screen. "Congratulations."

He entered something on the computer then checked the paper next to the keyboard.

Alexa stared at the top of his head. Her hands clenched in her lap. Although he'd said all the right words, the tone conveyed a coldness that left her chilled. She crossed her arms over her chest. "Is that all you have to say?" *Please tell me not to accept it because you—*

His gaze riveted to hers. "What else do you want me to say? That I wish you hadn't gotten the scholarship? That I wanted you to struggle to pay for your schooling? That I didn't want you to fulfill one of your dreams? What kind of man do you think I am?"

The kind I could fall in love with. She swallowed several times and said, "Well, no, but I would have liked to discuss the scholarship with you. I have to accept it by next Friday."

"Why wouldn't you accept it? It will give you the means to travel and teach in another country. It will pay for your last year of college and your student loans. You're young. You've got your whole life ahead of you, and this is a terrific opportunity for you."

His logical reasoning struck her in the face as though he'd slapped her. No emotion in his voice. No emotion in his expression. *Ask me to stay. Give me another dream.* Those words slipped into her mind and stunned her. She'd known she was falling in love with him, but until now she'd thought she could stop the feeling from taking over her life. But no, it was entrenched in her now, to the point where it took priority over what she'd always thought she wanted. But it was obvious Ian didn't return those feelings.

She rose. "I wanted you to know. That's all. I'd better get back to Jana. She's finishing up writing her own fairy tale and illustrating it. She wants to give it to her mother when she sees her tomorrow."

"Fine," he mumbled, and stared at the figures on the paper before him. *I care a great deal for Alexa, but I can't stand in her way.*

He waited until Alexa closed the office door before looking up. He didn't know how long he could conceal his true feelings. In his heart he'd known she would get the scholarship. *Why, Lord, did You send her to us and then take her away? Why is Tracy coming back now of all times? Alexa says You're her strength and I can rely on You for help. I need that help now. I feel my life is in shambles. About the only thing going right is Jana's recovery, but even that is threatened now with Tracy's visit.*

His eyes stung from exhaustion. He buried his face in his hands, massaging his fingertips into his skin. He would never give his heart to another. It hurt too much.

The next afternoon when the doorbell chimed, Jana raced into the foyer ahead of Ian. Alexa stayed in the kitchen and cleaned up after their lunch. An eruption of voices from the entryway broke into the silence that hung over the room while they had eaten. Her hand clenched around the dishrag she used to wipe the counters.

Lord, please be with Jana and Ian during this visit. Help both of them deal with their emotions concerning Tracy.

"Alexa, I want you to meet my mom," Jana said as she hugged a beautiful woman who looked like an older version of her.

Alexa stepped forward with her hand extended. "It's nice to meet you."

"Jana has told me you're tutoring her."

Although it wasn't a question, Alexa said, "Yes." Her mouth went dry at Tracy's assessing perusal. "Until tax season's over." She peered behind the woman and caught sight of Ian hanging back by the doorway into the kitchen, an unreadable expression on his face, his countenance of late.

"You mean when Ian decides to rejoin the living." Tracy's mouth pinched into a frown as she spun toward him. "In fact, I'm sure you have work to do right now. Don't let us keep you from it."

He lounged against the door frame with his arms folded over his chest. "Oh, that's okay. Don't worry about me." Although daggers didn't fly from his eyes, his voice held them.

Tracy stiffened, glared at him then rotated back to Jana. "Where's that dog of yours? Sugar?"

"I put her in my bedroom. I know you don't like pets."

"It's not that I don't like them, but I have an allergy to dog and cat fur." Tracy took Jana's hand. "Show me that fairy tale you wrote." She led her daughter toward the den.

Alexa watched them a few seconds until they disappeared into the other room, then she looked back at Ian, who remained by the entrance, all the nonchalance gone from his posture, his expression not unreadable now. She saw a man hurting. She crossed to him. "I'm here if you need to talk."

"I feel like…" He pressed his lips together.

"Like what?"

"Nothing. It's not important. I'll be in my office." He pivoted and strode away.

The urge to go after him and take him into her arms deluged Alexa as though hundreds of gallons of water drenched her. She took several steps toward him. As if sensing her behind him, he halted and peered over his shoulder.

"I'll be all right once she's gone."

His tone dismissed any help she might offer, and he continued the trek to his office. The sound of the door closing reinforced how easy it was for him to shut her out. Like her father had done for years. But not anymore. Could she break through Ian's defenses?

If he didn't want her help, then she could at least be here for Jana if she needed her. Alexa went back into the kitchen and decided to prepare something for dinner. She had to do something to keep herself busy while she listened to the chattering between Jana and her mother coming from the den.

Later that day, Alexa sat on Jana's bed as the young girl twirled around and held out the flowing material of her skirt. "You look beautiful in the new outfit your mother gave you. How do you feel about going to dinner with your mother and stepfather?"

Ian's daughter crunched her forehead. "I don't know. She wants to spend as much time with me as possible before she leaves on Sunday." She averted her gaze for a long moment. "But I never thought of her husband as my stepfather. I only have one dad."

"I agree and he does a great job." Even though he was stressed with the situation at the moment.

"I'm glad you stayed. He may need someone to talk to after I leave."

The child's concern for Ian touched Alexa deeply. In a lot of ways she was much older than her eleven years, especially with what she had gone through the past year. "I'll try to help any way I can." She could remember when Ian talked with her concerning her father. She wanted to return the favor, if he would allow her. But this was the first time he'd come face-to-face with his ex-wife since she left, and he was struggling with having any kind of closure. Would she be a help or a hindrance?

Jana placed her hand over her stomach. "I have butterflies."

"You're only a phone call away. And you all are going

to the restaurant at the inn. You like that place. You've been doing so good going places, even without your dad."

"And this is important. Then tomorrow Mom said we're going shopping. She loves to shop."

"Do you?"

Jana thought about it for a long moment. "No."

"Have you told your mother you'd rather do something else while she's here?"

"No. She's different. I'm not sure she's happy. Oh, she laughs and talks a lot, but something's wrong. I don't want to upset her."

"It's okay to express your wants. She's here for you. She came to Tallgrass because of you, remember that."

"Yeah, you're right. She promised me today to call more often, but I'm gonna try not to count on it."

"Why?" Alexa rose.

"Because I don't like how I feel when I get let down. I get so sad then angry at my mom. Do you think she left because of me?"

"No. You had nothing to do with it."

"I don't like being angry at her, because I'm afraid she won't call again or see me, but she hurt me." Tears misted in Jana's eyes.

"Honey, anytime you want to talk I'm here to listen. I had those same feelings with my dad."

Jana sucked in a shuddering breath. "What did you do?"

"Prayed a lot and worked to forgive him. Your mother wouldn't have come to see you if she didn't care."

"My counselor's been helping me to learn to count on myself."

"And the Lord."

"Yes, He's always here." Jana covered the space between them and hugged Alexa. "I love you, Alexa."

Her heart swelled, and her own love clogged her throat. "I love you, too. You're such a special young lady. Anyone would be proud to call you their daughter."

"I wish that you'd—" Jana snapped her mouth closed.

Alexa stepped back. "What?"

"Oh, nothing." The child grinned. "I think I'll wait on the front porch. She should be here any minute."

The doorbell rang as Jana left her bedroom. Alexa followed her to the foyer while Ian came out of his office.

The desolate look in his eyes vanished when he saw Jana. "Are you ready, pumpkin?"

His daughter nodded.

"If you need me, just call. I can be there in ten minutes. Are you sure you want to do this?"

"Yes. I'm gonna be fine, Dad. Don't worry about me." Jana pointedly peered at Alexa as Ian swung the front door open.

Tracy smiled at Jana. "That outfit looks great on you. We'll have to get some more like that tomorrow."

Jana slid her glance again toward Alexa for a few seconds then back to her mother. "I've been thinking about that. Can we do something else besides shopping?"

Tracy frowned. "Like what?"

"I haven't been to the Tallgrass Prairie Preserve lately. We could have a picnic there."

"Let's go. We've got a reservation at six-thirty. We'll talk about it at dinner." Tracy held out her hand.

Jana's huge gaze latched on to her father's for a long moment before she fit her quivering hand into her mother's. Jana was taking a big step tonight. Meeting outside the home with the person who had brought all her fears to the foreground. All Alexa wanted to do was wrap her arms around the young girl and tell her she loved her.

"You've got my cell phone." Ian kissed his daughter's cheek, a nerve twitching above his jaw.

Jana waved to her father as she walked beside her mother to the car waiting in the driveway. Ian stood on the porch, his hands stuffed into the pockets of his slacks. The stiff set to his shoulders and back underscored his tension. When the car disappeared from view, he turned to go into the house.

The bleakness he'd masked earlier took over his expression as his gaze fastened to Alexa's. "You don't have to stay."

"I promised Jana I would."

"I knew it. She's worried about being gone with her mother."

"Not exactly. Although I think she's a little anxious, she's mainly concerned about you."

"Why? I'm not the one who stopped going out because of her anxiety."

But you haven't moved on yet. "She thinks her mother leaving you all has affected you, too. Maybe even worse."

"Nonsense." Ian waved off her apprehension as he shut the front door. "I'm fine."

"Are you?"

He started to say something, but Alexa held up her hand to stop the words. "Think about what you've been feeling since you found out Tracy was coming to see Jana before you give me your stock answer that you're okay."

In three strides he closed the space between them. "What if my *stock* answer is right?"

"Is it?"

"It—it—" He jerked away and stalked toward his office.

Alexa followed. In the past month her dreams had been filled with pictures of her, Ian and Jana as a family, but she knew it was impossible. Ian was still in love with his wife. Anger and hate could be a mask to cover up his suppressed love. They had been married for over ten years. "So, it isn't right? You having some problems with Tracy being here?"

He whirled around in the middle of the room, his hands fisted at his sides. "You bet I am."

The lethally quiet words hung in the air between them, charging it with his intensity. His eyes narrowed on her face, but she kept her gaze unwavering. Her chin went up a notch.

"At least you're now admitting what I've known and obviously your daughter has for the past few weeks. Do you want to talk about it?"

"Why do women always want to talk about their feelings? No, I don't want to talk. I want to forget Tracy even existed."

Do you really? Alexa took a step closer to Ian. "Why?"

"Why! How can you ask that? She walked out on me and Jana. How can a mother do that to her child? I can understand abandoning a husband—me—" he thumped his chest "—but she practically ignored her daughter for over a year." All pretenses faded from his posture, expression, tone of voice, to be replaced with his anger, directed at his ex-wife. "And now she's waltzing back into Jana's life like nothing is different and wants to pick up as though the past seventeen months didn't happen."

"You're worried Jana won't be able to handle this visit—or is it more about you not being able to handle Tracy's reappearance?"

Ian flexed his hands, then curled them into a tight ball, his knuckles whitening. "When she walked out, she gave up certain rights."

"Like what? The right to hurt you anymore?"

A storm brewed in the depths of his blue eyes. "How about Jana? Tracy says she'll call and talk to Jana every week now, but what happens when she grows tired of doing that? I'm the one who'll be left to pick up the pieces."

"Give your daughter some credit. We talked. She understands her mother better now than you think, and when she doesn't, she has you."

"Doesn't stop the hurt."

"Again, for her or you?"

"I'm past the hurt. I'm angry at her for what she did to my daughter. Forget about me."

It would be easier if she could forget about him, but she couldn't. Alexa moved even closer, although his anger blasted the short space between them. "But you are tied up in this. This anger is controlling you. For a person who has desperately tried to control his life, you're letting your ex-wife run it."

"I am not…" He swallowed the rest of the sentence, glanced away for a moment before reestablishing eye contact with Alexa. The look bore into her.

"Forgive her. Let your anger go. If you don't, she will always be in control. Is that what you really want?"

"She betrayed me. Had an affair. Left without a word. Had little to do with Jana for over a year until now."

"I know and I didn't say it was gonna be easy. In fact, it might be one of the hardest things you ever do. Aren't you the one who helped me through what happened between my father and me?"

"This is different."

"Is it really? The anger consuming you is the same. And the way to fix it is the same." She splayed her hand over her chest. "Take it from someone who knows and has gone through it recently. Once I forgave my father, I felt such a peace and freedom from the past. The Lord can help you through it."

"I prayed for help when Tracy left. I didn't get an answer."

"Maybe you did get an answer, but it wasn't what you wanted to hear."

He drew himself up into a warrior stance—his arms held slightly away from his body, his shoulders thrust back, his head held high. "What your father did only affected you. What Tracy did affects Jana, too, not just me."

"That's an excuse to continue to hold on to your anger. I think your daughter actually feels sorry for her mother."

"She said that?"

"Jana doesn't think Tracy's really happy."

"She isn't?" He lowered his gaze, masking it from Alexa. *Is that hope in his voice?* Her heart ached at the thought she'd lost Ian for good today. The few kisses they'd shared were only because he was on the rebound. She'd never accept a relationship that couldn't be one hundred percent. "Your daughter is very perceptive. She thinks her mother is trying too hard to appear happy."

"I have a hard time having any empathy for Tracy when I remember my daughter's tears, questions and anxiety. How can I forget that first time Jana fell apart and refused to leave the house, all the times she clung to me in fear I would abandon her too? No matter what I told her about how I would never leave her, that I knew what that was like, she still didn't believe me—not at first. It's taken almost a year of therapy to get her to where she now goes out without me."

"I'm not saying you should forget. I'm saying you should forgive. Those two things are different and don't have to go hand in hand."

The rigidity of his stance collapsed, and he sank back against the front of his desk right behind him. He gripped its edge. "What if Tracy wants to take Jana? Wants joint custody? What if this visit is leading up to that?"

"Is that what you're really afraid of—losing Jana?"

He blew a breath out and nodded. "The courts seem to favor mothers over fathers, especially where a daughter is concerned."

"You have full custody of her now?" She'd never asked that question, just assumed.

"Yes. Tracy didn't want it."

"I know weird things can happen, but I don't think you need to worry. You've been there for Jana for seventeen months. You didn't leave her. That's got to count for something. And besides, Jana will never forget that. She loves you."

"I know, but—"

"Don't worry about something that probably won't ever happen. It's wasted energy."

"That's easy to say. You aren't a parent."

She really tried not to let his words hurt her. He was right. She wasn't a mother, but she knew what worrying did to a person. As a teen she'd lived a life of worry. "You're right. I'm not, but I care deeply for Jana." *And you.* But she would never share that with him. "Talk to Tracy. Find out what's going on before you let this worry eat you up. And pray for guidance."

Before Ian could reply, the phone cut into the silence. He jerked around and snatched up the receiver, a frown descending over his features. "Hello." There was a long pause then he said, "A movie? When will you be home?" His scowl deepened. "Fine. I'll see you at ten-thirty then." When he hung up, his hand lingered on the phone as he stared down at the desk.

"Jana's going to the movies with her mother?"

"Yeah."

"How did she sound?"

"Okay. She's been wanting to see this movie and said something to Tracy. That's when her mother thought it would be fun to see it together."

"And you don't like it?"

He lifted his head and stabbed her with a razor-sharp look. "No, I'd wanted to take her to see it after the fifteenth, when I had more time."

"There will be other movies." After she spoke, she realized how hollow those words sounded to a man hurting and struggling with his emotions concerning his ex-wife who had deserted him. "Tell you what, why don't I fix us something for dinner while you get some of the work you need to do finished. I'll come get you when I've got it prepared. Okay?"

A war of conflicting feelings—anger, sadness and resignation—paraded across his features. Finally resignation won out. "Fine."

Alexa left Ian as he sat behind his desk. While she closed the door to the office, she peeked in and glimpsed him scrubbing his hands down his face as though trying to keep himself alert after many sleepless nights. In that moment she wanted more than anything for him to love her, but she knew it wasn't going to happen, that she needed to move on, think about her dream and her future. She would call the Christian Teachers International Organization on Monday and accept the scholarship.

Chapter Twelve

"Did you have a nice time at the Tallgrass Prairie Preserve?" Ian asked as he let Jana and Tracy into the house late Saturday afternoon.

"Yeah, I saw several buffalo calves. They were so cute." Jana's cheeks were rosy from too much sun.

Didn't Tracy see their daughter needed some sunscreen? Ian gritted his teeth to keep his criticism to himself. His ex-wife was leaving tomorrow morning, and he couldn't be happier. He hated this disruption to their life. Jana and he were doing just fine before she'd come back as though nothing happened. Probably not even aware of what their daughter had really gone through with her leaving.

Sugar bounded into the foyer, tail wagging as she leaped up and down. Jana scooped her pet up into her arms. "I'd better go feed her. Will ya stay a little while, Mom?"

"I need to talk to your father then I'll come find you. Okay?"

Jana glanced from him to her mother. "Yeah." His daughter's gaze lit upon him again, and she hesitated, but

Sugar wiggled so much in her arms she released her dog and quickly hurried after the yelping animal.

"What do you want?" Ian brought his attention back to Tracy.

"Let's talk somewhere private."

That didn't bode well. A tightening in his gut increased its grip as he strode toward his office and gestured for Tracy to go inside first. Why did he feel as if he was walking to his doom? He closed the door, faced the woman who had betrayed him and waited for her to say something.

She scanned the room. "This has a more lived-in look than your office where you worked downtown."

He stiffened. "Is that what you wanted to point out, the difference in the decor of my two offices?"

"No, not really. Just an observation." She sauntered to the couch and sat. "Please have a seat. It's been a long day, and we did a lot of walking. I would have preferred to go shopping, but oh, well." After sliding to one end, she patted the cushion. "You haven't loosened up a bit this past year, have you? Sit."

A thought invaded Ian's mind. Tracy sounded like Jana teaching Sugar a dog trick. The implication raised the heat in his blood. He remained standing. "I've been sitting all day. I'm fine just like this."

"Suit yourself. You always have."

"If all we're going to do is exchange barbs, I think this conversation is at an end." He started for the door.

"I want Jana to come visit me this summer in Arizona."

Halting in midstride, he closed his eyes, trying to picture anything that would calm his rapidly skyrocketing temper. An image of Alexa popped into his mind. For a few seconds her smile filled him with serenity.

"Ian, did you hear me?"

Tracy's grating tone scraped down his spine, and he went rigid as he pivoted toward her. "Excuse me."

"I want Jana to visit me. We can go see some of the sights around there. I know she'd love the Grand Canyon."

"You know? How? You haven't spent much time with her."

"I want to change that. People can do that even if you haven't. You're the same rigid man I married twelve years ago and thought I could change."

Her comment made him vividly aware of his stiff stance that supported exactly what she'd said. He forced himself to relax his posture although he couldn't unfurl his hands.

"You never wanted to do anything fun. All you did was work. I poured my heart into decorating this house, and you hardly said a word. And when you did have time, you wanted to spend it all as a family."

"I was trying to earn a living to support your decorating trips to Dallas and Kansas City with your friends."

She held up her hand. "I didn't come here to discuss our past. It's over. I've come to the conclusion you can't change any man." A frown twisted her mouth.

"A woman can change, but a man can't?"

"Exactly."

"Why did you come back after all this time?"

"To see my daughter."

"Why didn't you before now?"

"I—I…" Tracy peered away, biting her lower lip. "Jana and I talked today, and I'm gonna do better. I was wrong not to. I was trying to make my new marriage work. It required all my time and energy."

"It isn't working?"

"No. Sam is okay, and I know he loves me—" she threw

him a pointed look "—which is more than I could have said for you, but I don't think I'm meant to be married."

"Have you told Sam?" Strangely, he should feel vindicated and elated at what was happening to Tracy. He didn't, which surprised him.

"No, I'm not going to give up. I'm going to work at my marriage. That's one of the reasons we took this cross-country trip."

"Why didn't you work at our marriage? You never talked to me about what you were really feeling."

"Feelings? Do you have any?"

He ground his teeth together. If the pain he'd experienced was any indication, his emotions were alive and well.

"You're so reserved. Everything had a place, even me."

All he wanted was to end this conversation. "Jana has had a hard time since you left. Did you even know your daughter is seeing a therapist? I'm not uprooting her and sending her halfway across the country to visit you. You're free to come here if you want." And he meant that, which was another surprise to him. He continued his trek to the door and thrust it open, relishing the fresh air that seemed to rush into the heated atmosphere in his office. "Just give me notice. Good night, Tracy."

Glaring at him, she shot to her feet. "Do we have to go back to court?"

"Do what you feel you need to." He stared straight ahead. *I refuse to worry about it anymore. I will deal with it when or if it happens. Alexa's right. I can't control her actions.*

Tracy walked to him. "Look, I'll admit I handled our situation all wrong. I know that. I've already admitted I should have contacted Jana more often, but—"

"Sending her a present on special occasions isn't really

contact, Tracy. She needed to hear your voice. She needed to understand why you abandoned her."

"Abandoned her? I left her in your care while I tried to figure out what I wanted in life. I was a mess to be around. She didn't need to see that."

He raised one brow. "And did you figure it out as you rushed into another marriage?"

"I'm working on it." Tears gleamed in her eyes.

"Oh, don't you dare start crying and think that's going to control me."

"I never thought I could control you. You do such a good job of that yourself."

Control? He had little of that. This visit hammered home that fact.

Ian glanced down the hallway, heard his daughter in the kitchen and stepped back into the office, closing the door so she wouldn't hear their conversation, which obviously wasn't over. "Yes, you thought you could control me. I went to work for that big accounting firm downtown that you just complained I worked for all the time. I did it because you wanted me to when I wanted to open my own office. Maybe I wouldn't have made as much money, but I would have been able to spend more time with you and Jana."

"Jana! You were always thinking about her."

"She's our daughter. Why wouldn't I? We were a family."

"I wanted some of that time." She pointed to herself. "I needed to feel like I was the most important person in your life."

"This wasn't a competition between you and Jana. I loved you two equally." In that moment he realized he didn't love Tracy anymore—hadn't in over a year. That his anger had come from what had happened to Jana and the fact he hadn't been able to control anything that occurred concerning Tracy.

Tracy's mouth pinched together. She reached for the door. "It wasn't enough. I want to see Jana more. Don't make this difficult for everyone."

Tracy stalked toward the den. Ian hurried after her, afraid of what his ex-wife would do or say to Jana.

Lord, I need Your help. What am I supposed to do?

Stopping inside the entrance, Tracy plastered a huge smile on her face. "Honey, I wanted to give you another hug before I leave."

Jana tossed a small ball for Sugar, then rose from the floor and headed for her mother. "I had fun today. Thanks, Mom."

Tracy took Jana into her arms and planted a kiss on the top of her daughter's head. "I'll call you when I get back home. I want us to spend more time together in Phoenix. I'm hoping your dad—" she tossed a piercing glance at Ian "—will allow it."

Ian tensed, wishing he'd never let the woman into the house. This day couldn't get any worse.

"Dad?" Jana turned toward him.

"We'll talk about it later," was all he could think of to say to his daughter, whose eyes searched his face with accusation in them.

"We can have such fun when you come." His ex-wife gave Jana another quick hug, clasped Jana's hand and strode toward the foyer with his daughter.

After months of working to get Jana in a place where she could heal, was all that going to be destroyed with one visit from Tracy? Ian shook the question from his mind and quickly trailed after the pair.

Lord, where are You?

At the front door Tracy placed her hands on Jana's shoulders. "I'm thinking the first of June. It'll be hot but not as bad as July and August. We have a pool, so you can swim when we aren't going places." After a kiss on his daughter's cheek, Tracy left.

Left him to face Jana.

Left him to explain why he didn't want his daughter to fly by herself to Phoenix and see Tracy. What if she never returned to Tallgrass? What if she preferred living with her mom and stepfather? Panic attacked his insides, twisting his gut into a huge knot. It was all he could do to remain in the entry hall. Tracy had abandoned him without giving him a chance to fix things, and now even Alexa would be leaving after she graduated in December. He couldn't deal with his daughter leaving, too.

Please, Lord, help me. What do I do?

"Dad, are you all right?"

Jana's question, spoken with concern not anger, reined in his spiraling panic. "No. I—I don't want you to go in June."

"Why?"

It's too soon. You have so much more healing to do. I don't want to lose you.

"We need to talk with your therapist about this. I'm not sure it's a good idea after the past year. I'll go with you to your next session and see what she thinks." It was a cop-out, but he didn't know what else to do. "Did you really have a good time?"

Jana looked at him for a long moment. "Yes, but I would rather have gone with you and Alexa. Maybe we can go back after the fifteenth. I know that Alexa would love the fields of wildflowers. One reminded me of a skirt she wears a lot."

The image flashed into his mind of Alexa in the skirt that his daughter was talking about. A smile graced Alexa's lips. A twinkle danced in her eyes. His heart slowed to a throb. After this encounter with Tracy, he knew that he couldn't commit to anyone else until he figured out the mess his life had become. The fury he'd felt today had consumed him, taking all his peace and contentment and destroying it. He couldn't keep going on like this.

Was it as simple as Alexa said? Forgive Tracy—let go of the hurt and hate that controlled his life? In that moment he felt his life was out of his control, crumbling piece by piece and shattering all around him.

"Daddy, I love you." Jana threw her arms around him.

He relished the hug from his daughter and her words. "I love you, pumpkin."

The sound of the phone echoed through the house. "I'll get this in my office." If it was Tracy wanting to talk some more about Jana visiting her, he didn't want his daughter overhearing the conversation.

On the fifth ring he grabbed the receiver on his desk. "Hello."

"How did everything go today with Jana and her mother?"

Hearing the soft lilt of Alexa's voice soothed him. He sank into his chair. He closed his eyes and relished the connection with her, if only for a brief time. "She had a good time, but Tracy stayed to talk to me about Jana visiting her in June in Arizona."

"Did you agree?"

"No. I don't want her to go."

"Does Jana know about the invitation?"

"Yes. Her mother made sure of that." A bitter taste coated his tongue.

"How does Jana feel about going?"

Ian's clasp tightened around the phone. "I think she'd like to. I don't think she wants to disappoint her mother. Too bad Tracy didn't think about her daughter like that."

"What are you going to do?"

"Alexa, I don't know. I told Jana I would talk with her therapist about this, but I don't want her to go."

"What are you afraid will happen?"

Afraid? His thoughts came to a grinding halt.

"Ian?"

"I'm still here." He sucked in a breath. "Losing Jana."

"You won't. She loves you. Do you want me to come over? We can talk this through if you need a sounding board."

"No." He bit the word out through clenched teeth. He couldn't deal with seeing her beautiful face right now. *I love you, Alexa.* And for that reason he didn't want her to see him grappling with his whole life, trying to find a solution to his problems and get his life back on track.

"Okay, I'll see you two at church tomorrow."

"We won't be there. Tracy is coming by for breakfast with Jana tomorrow before she and her husband head out of town." It had been set up before the bombshell from Tracy, or he would never have agreed to Tracy coming over tomorrow morning. "Jana wants to fix it. Show her mom what she's learned from you."

"Then I'll be at your house Monday morning bright and early."

When he hung up, he clutched the arms of his chair and stared straight ahead. *Lord, if You have a solution, please clue me in. I'm lost. I don't know what to do anymore.*

No brilliant idea came to mind. Nothing.

His attention swung to the pile of work on his desk. He knew sleep would evade him, so he decided to complete as much work as he could tonight. Keep himself busy so he didn't have to think of the chaos he felt his life had become. He loved a woman he shouldn't. The realization struck him with a gut-wrenching punch because Alexa deserved so much more from a man than he could give. Listening to her tonight firmed that in his mind. He needed to let her go to do what she'd dreamed of. She was young and in a different place than he was. He had obligations and commitments while she didn't. He had Jana to think about, while Alexa was free to do what she wanted.

For the next hour Ian tried to concentrate on the tax forms he was filling out for a client, but his mind wandered. Every time he got a new e-mail he checked it, anything not to work. When he saw that Alexa sent him a message, he gave up pretending, especially after he read her email.

I was reading my Bible before going to bed, preparing for a lesson tomorrow in my Sunday-school class. This verse leaped off the page, and I knew I had to send it to you. It's from Ephesians' fourth chapter. "And be ye kind one to another, tenderhearted, forgiving one another, even as God for Christ's sake hath forgiven you." I hope that helps you through your dilemma.

The verse stuck in his mind and wouldn't let him go. Over and over it played through his thoughts as though the Lord had sent him a personal message—an answer to his problems. *Forgive Tracy. Let go of the anger controlling you—causing you to live in the past.*

Alexa had only e-mailed him one other time—a link to a homeschooling site she'd found on the Internet. That had been two months ago. He didn't believe in coincidences. Earlier he'd asked for help. Was this it?

Ian shut down the computer and went in search of his Bible. He needed to do some reading and soul-searching tonight. He knew he couldn't continue as he was—so full of anger toward Tracy that he was powerless to move forward. This wasn't how he wanted to live, and he would start with the verse Alexa sent him.

When Ian opened the door for Alexa on Monday morning, a smile curved his mouth and hope blossomed in her. Saturday night on the spur of the moment she had sent him that Bible verse, but hadn't talked to him since then. She'd almost called him several times yesterday, but had refrained, although it had been one of the hardest things she'd done.

"How's everything?" *What happened yesterday with breakfast? Did you and Tracy talk anymore?* She squeezed her lips together to keep those questions inside.

"Better."

Okay. She couldn't keep totally quiet. "How did breakfast go with Tracy?"

"I told her Jana could come see her if the therapist thought it would be all right, but that I would accompany my daughter. We would stay in a hotel near her house and would take it slow and easy. I don't want my daughter backsliding." He glanced toward the kitchen then back at Alexa. "I took what you sent me to heart. I can't keep going on being angry at Tracy. I let it go yesterday."

"And how do you feel?"

He blinked as though he hadn't really stopped and thought about his feelings since doing it. "Frankly, good. As though I'm free. I know there will be days when I'll still struggle, but I don't want my past to control my life anymore. I didn't like what was happening to me with Tracy's appearance, the anger that consumed me."

"Good." He'd taken a big step forward. Her hope mushroomed even more. Maybe they had a chance. She wanted that, and yet she had to let the people at the foundation know if she was going to accept the scholarship. She needed to talk to Ian about it.

Jana came from the kitchen, munching on a piece of toast with grape jelly. "Alexa, I found some more goose eggs this morning when I was outside with Sugar. Two of them built a nest in our yard under the bushes near the water."

"How neat! You'll be able to follow their progress. Let's make that the next animal you study."

"Way ahead of you. I've already gone online to find out more about geese. Come on into the den and I'll show you."

"I'll be with you in a few minutes. I need to talk to your dad about something."

Jana glanced from her to her father then back to her, a twinkle in her eye. "Oh, take your time. It'll give me a chance to find out more information."

The little matchmaker was at work again, Alexa thought with a smile. When the child left, she turned to Ian and said, "Let's talk in your office."

"This sounds serious. Is something wrong?"

Alexa walked toward the room. "Well, no, not exactly."

When he entered behind her, he closed the door. "Is it about the scholarship? Have you accepted it?"

"Not yet. I have until the sixteenth." *Give me a reason to stay in Tallgrass. I love you.*

"You need to."

It wasn't a question, and although his expression was neutral, his tone of voice held resignation. She nodded. "I know, but…" She couldn't say the rest out loud.

"Why wouldn't you tell them yes? This is a great opportunity."

She had to seize the moment and see if they had a chance together. She would regret it if she didn't say something. "I could stay if I thought you and me…" Again her words trailed off as she stared into his face, a shutter descending over his features. She'd never struggled so much to say what was on her mind. The stakes were high, and yet she was at a loss as to what to say.

"No, you were meant to go. This is your dream. You can't turn your back on it."

"I thought the past few months a relationship—I mean, you kissed me," she finally said when she couldn't quite say what she was really feeling.

When he was agitated, he would rake his hand through his hair, which was what he did right now. "We shared a few kisses and I really like you, but you need to do this for yourself. My home is here. Yours is somewhere else." He threw a glance over his shoulder at the work stacked on his desk. "I need to finish some tax preparation for my clients. It's only a few days to the deadline."

"Yeah, sure." Alexa pivoted toward the door. Her deadline was a few days away, too.

Before she left, Ian said, "Please don't tell Jana. Let me explain to her that you got the scholarship."

"All right," she murmured with her back to him. Then she hurried from the office before she broke down and cried. She'd all but told him she'd wanted to stay because of him. And he'd told her to go.

"Jana, I need to talk with you." Ian sat on the couch next to his daughter in the den.

She put down her paper and pencil on the end table next to her. "Is it about going to see Mom?"

"Well, no, but since your therapist okayed it today, I'll let your mom know we'll be there the first week in June. But at any time during the visit, if you feel anxious and upset, I need to know." Although, after over a year, he knew Jana's signs when she was becoming agitated, and he wouldn't hesitate to step in and cut the trip short if he had to for his daughter.

"I will. I've been looking into some places we could go while we're out there. Did you know there are some great Indian ruins not too far from Phoenix?"

"No, but maybe we could drive out there and see some things along the way." He'd much rather delve into the various sightseeing opportunities than talk to his daughter about Alexa leaving, but he couldn't postpone it any longer. He'd already waited four days until they had gone to the therapist. He'd wanted to get the visit with her mother settled before telling Jana Alexa got the scholarship and would leave Tallgrass at the end of the year. That she would be gone for at least three years—possibly longer.

"What do you want to talk to me about?"

Jana's question focused him on what he had to do, although his gut knotted into a huge ball. He drew in a fortifying breath and said, "Alexa got the scholarship she'd applied for. She's already making plans to go to school full-time in the summer and next fall. She'll graduate next December."

"And leave Tallgrass after that?"

He nodded, his throat tight. When he'd told Alexa she couldn't turn down the chance to fulfill a dream, he hadn't told her how he'd come to love her. He didn't want to stand in her way, but keeping those words inside had been the hardest thing he'd done in a long time. The urge to grab her and hold her against him, keep her near, had inundated him Monday evening when they'd talked about the scholarship.

Jana dropped her head, grasping her hands in her lap. "Why does she have to leave?"

"Because that's part of accepting the money to finish

school. She has to fulfill the obligation of teaching in an underdeveloped country for three years. She wants to do it."

"But what about you two? I saw ya kiss her. Don't ya want her to stay? Don't ya care about her?"

"Yes, I care about Alexa. I love…" He couldn't finish saying the words. When he said them aloud, it would be real. Not that it wasn't real now.

"I knew you did! I knew it!" Jana grinned from ear to ear. "Now all ya have to do is tell her."

His feelings for Alexa had snuck up on him. She'd become important to him when he wasn't looking. But he couldn't stop her from doing what she wanted, had dreamed about since she was in high school. Alexa needed to do this before she settled down with a family of her own. But the thought of her with another man burned a hole in his gut.

"Jana, I know you care about Alexa and don't want her to leave, but sometimes we have to do things for people we lo—care about for them, not us. Who knows? Maybe she'll come back to Tallgrass." Although he doubted it—three years would change her and her feelings. On Monday she'd indicated she cared for him, but she was only twenty-three. Those feelings would change once she was away from Tallgrass. She'd forget about him.

Jana turned totally toward him, a gleam in her eyes. "We could go with her. That would be perfect. We could see the world, help others."

Stunned by his daughter's suggestion, Ian just stared at her, her words swirling around in his mind. Leave Tallgrass? His home for almost half his life? Where he had his business? Where he knew what to expect most of the time?

"Pumpkin, it isn't that simple."

Her mouth a thin line, she straightened. "Why not?"

"It just isn't." He rose, a picture of him, Alexa and Jana trekking all over the world, one unknown adventure after another. His daughter needed stability. He needed stability. Didn't he? "I've got a few things I need to take care of in the office, then you and I can go out to dinner if you want."

"Sure," Jana mumbled, her head down again.

Ian escaped into his office and stared at his desk, neat now. In order. Like his life?

There was nothing that felt as if he was in control. In fact, he felt the opposite ever since Alexa stormed into his life. She'd swept away all the old perceptions he'd had about what he wanted. But this wasn't about what he wanted. It was all about what Alexa wanted. Wasn't that why he hadn't said anything to her Monday evening? Hadn't pleaded with her to stay?

He sat for a moment at his desk, glancing around at his life as he rapped his fingers against the arm of his chair. What if he gave all this up? Took Jana and went with Alexa?

No, he couldn't. He surged to his feet. He couldn't sit another moment. Marching from his office, he went to his bedroom and dug his jogging clothes out. After quickly donning them, he found Madge in the kitchen with Jana.

"I'm going for a run. I'll be back in an hour or so. If you need me, I have my cell."

"Fine," Jana mumbled while she hovered over her glass of milk and dunked a chocolate cookie into it. She didn't look up at him.

Outside, Ian set a fast pace, anything to drive away the thoughts spiraling out of control in his head. No matter how hard he pushed himself, he couldn't rid his mind that Alexa was the best thing that had happened to him. She made him feel alive. She made him realize it was okay if not everything went according to his plans.

Lord, I don't know if I could drop everything and leave Tallgrass to go overseas—even to help others, to be with Alexa. I love her, but I would be uprooting Jana…and me.

As he started to cross the street, a screeching sound reverberated through the air. He stopped and looked toward where the noise came from. A car came barreling around the corner. He jumped back as it sped past him. In a blink of an eye, everything could have changed for him if he hadn't stopped when he did.

Life is a risk. You can't plan it. It has a way of throwing you a curve when you least expect it. Alexa's words came to mind, haunting him, mocking his need to control his circumstances. Had he been able to control Tracy leaving? Jana's problems? Only the Lord was in control and he needed to believe He had the best in mind for him and Jana.

His cell rang. He slowed down and pulled it out of his pocket. "Yes," he said, breathing hard, his lungs burning.

Madge's voice answered him. "Ian, Jana said she was going to her room. When I went to check on her, she wasn't in there, but I found a note on her bed. She left to go to Alexa's to talk with her."

He came to a halt and scanned the area. He was only five blocks away from Alexa's, as though he'd unknowingly planned to go see her.

"I'll take care of it. Thanks." Pocketing his cell, he jogged toward Alexa's duplex.

"Honey, how are things going in Tallgrass?" was the first thing her mom asked when she'd phoned right after Alexa had come in from class at six-thirty Thursday evening.

"Fine." *I should be on top of the world. I'm doing what I wanted. Then why do I feel so sad?*

"You can't fool me. You aren't doing fine."

"Mom, don't start with me." Alexa sank onto a chair in the kitchen.

"You didn't say anything to Ian about how you feel about him?"

"I told you I tried Monday night. I've hardly seen him this week. Remember, today is the fifteenth. A big day for a CPA. He's been busy."

"Then say something tomorrow. You're going to work tomorrow, aren't you?"

"Yes. My last day isn't until the end of April."

"Ah, he's keeping you around after the fifteenth. I wonder why."

"Because he has some things to do since he's been so focused on doing taxes these past months."

"Yeah, that's a good reason to keep you around." Her mother's chuckle taunted Alexa.

She gripped the mobile phone. The sound of the doorbell echoed through her house. "Someone's here. I'll talk to you later. Tell Dad hi for me. Bye."

After hanging up, Alexa hurried toward the foyer. When she opened the door, she blinked. "Jana, why are you here? Are you okay? Does your father know you are here?"

"I left him a note telling him I was coming over to talk to you."

Alexa stood to the side to allow Jana inside. "But he doesn't know?"

Jana shrugged.

"I need to call him and let him know you are here."

"Use his cell number. He's out jogging."

In the living room Alexa snatched up her phone and dialed Ian.

"Is Jana there?" he asked in a breathless voice before Alexa could say anything.

"Yeah."

"I'm a few minutes away from your place."

The thought of him coming to her house sent her heartbeat galloping. When she'd talked with her mother, she'd realized she needed to tell Ian point-blank how she felt about him. Then if he still wanted her to take the scholarship and leave, she would. But she had to risk it and let him know how important he was to her.

After putting the receiver back in its cradle, she swung around to face Jana. "Why did you come over to see me?"

"I wanted you to know that Dad loves you. You two belong together."

Dad loves you. Those words resonated through Alexa's mind. "Your father and I are friends, Jana. You shouldn't read anything else into it."

"It's more than that. He told me tonight."

"He did?" Alexa clasped her hands behind her back to keep the young girl from seeing how much they trembled. *He loves me. Is it Jana's wish or really true?*

"Yes, I'm not lying to you. He wants you to stay but won't tell you because he thinks you want to go. I came over to tell you. You two are making a big mistake."

"We are?" She couldn't think of anything else to say because out her front picture window she saw Ian jogging up the sidewalk. The sight of him doubled her pounding heartbeat.

Jana turned to see what Alexa was staring at. "Ask him." She gestured toward her dad coming to a stop on her porch. "Is Charlie out back?"

"Yes."

"I'm going to see him. Talk to Dad. Don't make the biggest mistake of your life." The young girl hurried toward the kitchen.

When Alexa opened the front door, Ian's gaze captured hers and held her for a long moment. All words fled her mind.

"I don't know what got into Jana's head. Leaving like that." Ian approached her, only a few inches separating them.

"She was upset about me going away." *Tell him how you feel. What do you have to lose now?* Monday she hadn't been as straightforward as she should have been. "She thinks we should be together, that you love me." When his eyes widened, she continued, "I love you, Ian, and whether I go or not, that won't change." *There. I've told him. If Jana is wrong, at least I've done what I needed to do.*

"You love me?"

"Yes. For the longest time I was sure you were still in love with your ex-wife, so I fought these feelings, but I can't any longer. Is Jana right? Do we have a chance?"

He started to reach for her then suddenly dropped his arms back to his sides. "You need to fulfill your dream. What if you stay and then down the line you regret never going? I couldn't live with that."

"Why can't we do it together? What's keeping you here? Jana could learn so much seeing firsthand places she's read about."

"The world as her classroom?"

"Well, at least for a few years. After that, who knows?"

He raked his hands through his hair, averting his gaze. "That's a big step. That's a—"

"A big change." Alexa moved even closer to him. "Yes, it is. I'd stay if it meant we had a chance. You mean too much to me."

He sucked in a breath. "I could never ask you to do that."

"You're not. Do we have a chance?"

His gaze locked with hers, a softening in his blue eyes

that rocked her clear to her toes. "I love you, Alexa, but this isn't about that."

"Yes, it is. I'm not taking the scholarship if that means I lose you. End of story. Dreams can be changed. I can help people here."

He shook his head and stepped away. "I can't let you give up on a dream like that."

"What's your dream?"

He moistened his lips. "To have a family—a wife I love, children. That's all I ever really wanted."

"Then let me give that to you."

"Not fair to you."

"Not having you in my life isn't fair to me. A place won't make me happy. But you can."

"I hate to fly."

Hope blossomed in her. "I can help you overcome your fear."

"It's a control thing."

"Will you give control to God?"

"Is that a trick question?"

"No."

His forehead crunched. "I know what you're doing. I know I don't really control my life like I used to think I do."

"Then we can work through that fear. If the Lord is with you, anything is possible—even flying."

He stared at her for a long moment, then suddenly dragged her against him, winding his arms around her. She cuddled into his embrace, relishing his warmth, his scent, his smile.

"The only way I see it working is if you take the scholarship and when you leave to fulfill your obligation, Jana and I go with you."

"Go with me? What are you saying?"

"I want us to be that family I've dreamed of." One corner

of his mouth lifted. "I help you with your dream. You help me with mine. A deal?"

"Marry you?" She looked up into his adoring gaze and never wanted to leave the shelter of his arms.

"Yes. You taught me to love again, to put my past behind me, but I'm thinking I'll need a lot of lessons to get it perfect. Do you think you could tutor me?"

She laughed and planted a kiss on his mouth. "You've got yourself a teacher—for life."

Epilogue

"Are you ready, Alexa?"

She took her father's arm. "Is this really happening?"

"Yes, in the next half an hour you'll become Mrs. Ian Ferguson. In case I haven't told you lately, I love you. You're going to make a wonderful wife for Ian."

"Let's do this." She grinned at her dad and moved toward the foyer of the church, wearing her mother's wedding dress.

There by the double doors into the sanctuary stood Jana waiting for her. As her maid of honor she wore a pale yellow dress of chiffon with tiny yellow roses woven throughout her hair. A beam lit the child's eyes, and she turned to enter as the music began.

Alexa took a deep breath and followed, feeling as though she glided toward her destiny. Ian watched her walk toward him, the sparkle in his blue eyes melting any doubts she might have had. She loved him with all her heart. Jana, too. She was finally going to have the family she always wanted.

When she stopped beside him, he moved close and leaned in to whisper, "I love you. There can't be a happier man alive today."

* * * * *

Dear Readers,

Love Lessons is the first in a three-book series about various situations involving homeschooling. I have many friends who have homeschooled their children. It has been fun exploring the different ways to homeschool. Although it isn't for everyone, it is definitely the answer for many families. I hope you will enjoy a glimpse into my fictional families who choose to homeschool their children.

I love hearing from readers. You can contact me at margaretdaley@gmail.com or at P.O. Box 2074, Tulsa, OK 74101. You can also learn more about my books at http://www.margaretdaley.com. I have a quarterly newsletter that you can sign up for on my Web site or you can enter my monthly drawings by signing my guest book on the Web site.

Best wishes,

Margaret Daley

QUESTIONS FOR DISCUSSION

1. Ian couldn't forgive his ex-wife for betraying him. His past ruled his life. Is there something that happened in your past that has done that to you? How can you get past that?

2. Who is your favorite character? Why?

3. Alexa's relationship with her father was rocky all her life. She had a lot of anger toward him because she had never felt he loved her. Do you or someone you know have a similar relationship with a parent? How have you or that parent dealt with that situation?

4. Ian didn't think the Lord answered his prayers. Have you ever thought that? If so, what did you do?

5. What is your favorite scene? Why?

6. Jana developed separation anxiety because her mother suddenly left her and her father. She was scared, especially that her father would leave her, too. Do you know anyone who experiences anxiety to the point that it governs how he/she lives? What are some things you can do to help that person get over his/her anxiety?

7. Ian thought if he could control his life he would be all right. He didn't realize there are a lot of things we can't control in our lives. What are some things that have happened to you lately that have been out of your control? How did you deal with them?

8. Alexa's mother left her husband because she didn't feel he appreciated her. Everything had to be his way. Have you ever been around someone like that? What were some things you did to handle that person?

9. Alexa's father dealt with his grief by pushing away everyone who loved him. How have you dealt with grief?

10. Although Alexa knew she should forgive her father, that God wanted her to, she couldn't. Have you ever done something you know you shouldn't? How did the situation turn out by avoiding what you knew you should do?

11. Ian was willing to let Alexa leave Tallgrass to fulfill her dream although he was in love with her. What are some situations where you've sacrificed your happiness for another?

12. Alexa's dream was changing as she got to know Ian and Jana. Has what you wanted for the future ever changed because of a situation or from getting to know someone? Do you think you are happier with the change in the direction your life took? Why or why not?

Here's a sneak peek at
THE WEDDING GARDEN
by Linda Goodnight,
the second book in her new miniseries
REDEMPTION RIVER,
available in May 2010 from Love Inspired.

One step into the living room and she froze again, pan aloft.

A hulking shape stood in shadow just inside the French doors leading out to the garden veranda. This was not Pop-bottle Jones. This was a big, bulky, dangerous-looking man. She raised the pan higher.

"What do you want?"

"Annie?" He stepped into the light.

All the blood drained from Annie's face. Her mouth went dry as saltines. "Sloan Hawkins?"

The man removed a pair of silver aviator sunglasses and hung them on the neck of his black rock-and-roll T-shirt. He'd rolled the sleeves up, baring muscular biceps. A pair of eyes too blue to define narrowed, looking her over as though he were a wolf and she a bunny rabbit.

Annie suppressed an annoying shiver.

It was Sloan, all right, though older and with more muscle. His nearly black hair was shorter now—no more bad-boy curl over the forehead—but bad boy screamed off him in waves just the same. He was devastatingly handsome, in a tough, rugged, manly kind of way. The years had been kind to Sloan Hawkins.

She really wanted to hate him, but she'd already wasted

too much emotion on this outlaw. With God's help she'd
learned to forgive. But she wasn't about to forget.

Will Sloan and Annie's faith be strong
enough to see them through
the pain of the past and allow them to open
their hearts to a possible future?
Find out in THE WEDDING GARDEN
by Linda Goodnight,
available May 2010 from Love Inspired.

Love Inspired

Former bad boy Sloan Hawkins is back in
Redemption, Oklahoma, to help keep his aunt's
cherished garden thriving and to reconnect with the
girl he left behind, Annie Markham. But when he
discovers his secret child—and that single mother
Annie never stopped loving him—he's determined
that a wedding will take place in the garden
nurtured by faith and love.

REDEMPTION
RIVER

Where healing flows...

Look for
The Wedding Garden
by Linda Goodnight

*Available May 2010
wherever you buy books.*

Steeple
Hill®

LI87595

www.SteepleHill.com

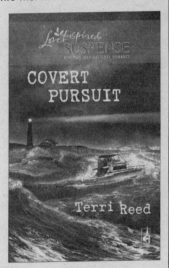

LARGER-PRINT BOOKS!

GET 2 FREE LARGER-PRINT NOVELS PLUS 2 FREE MYSTERY GIFTS

Larger-print novels are now available...

YES! Please send me 2 FREE LARGER-PRINT Love Inspired® novels and my 2 FREE mystery gifts (gifts are worth about $10). After receiving them, if I don't wish to receive any more books, I can return the shipping statement marked "cancel." If I don't cancel, I will receive 6 brand-new novels every month and be billed just $4.74 per book in the U.S. or $5.24 per book in Canada. That's a saving of over 20% off the cover price. It's quite a bargain! Shipping and handling is just 50¢ per book in the U.S. and 75¢ per book in Canada.* I understand that accepting the 2 free books and gifts places me under no obligation to buy anything. I can always return a shipment and cancel at any time. Even if I never buy another book, the two free books and gifts are mine to keep forever.

122 IDN E4KN 322 IDN E4KY

Name _____
(PLEASE PRINT)

Address _____ Apt. #

City _____ State/Prov. _____ Zip/Postal Code

Signature (if under 18, a parent or guardian must sign)

Mail to Steeple Hill Reader Service:
IN U.S.A.: P.O. Box 1867, Buffalo, NY 14240-1867
IN CANADA: P.O. Box 609, Fort Erie, Ontario L2A 5X3

**Are you a current subscriber to Love Inspired books
and want to receive the larger-print edition?
Call 1-800-873-8635 or visit www.morefreebooks.com.**

* Terms and prices subject to change without notice. Prices do not include applicable taxes. Sales tax applicable in N.Y. Canadian residents will be charged applicable provincial taxes and GST. Offer not valid in Quebec. This offer is limited to one order per household. All orders subject to approval. Credit or debit balances in a customer's account(s) may be offset by any other outstanding balance owed by or to the customer. Please allow 4 to 6 weeks for delivery. Offer available while quantities last.

Your Privacy: Steeple Hill Books is committed to protecting your privacy. Our Privacy Policy is available online at www.SteepleHill.com or upon request from the Reader Service. From time to time we make our lists of customers available to reputable third parties who may have a product or service of interest to you. If you would prefer we not share your name and address, please check here. ☐

Help us get it right—We strive for accurate, respectful and relevant communications. To clarify or modify your communication preferences, visit us at www.ReaderService.com/consumerschoice.

LILP10

TITLES AVAILABLE NEXT MONTH

Available April 27, 2010

THE WEDDING GARDEN
Redemption River
Linda Goodnight

WIFE WANTED IN DRY CREEK
Janet Tronstad

HOMETOWN PRINCESS
Lenora Worth

A DAUGHTER'S LEGACY
Virginia Smith

THE MARRIAGE MISSION
Pam Andrews

THE ROAD TO FORGIVENESS
Leigh Bale